"Mayday! Mayday! Attack waiting for Officer Leyton at the Truesch farm. Attempting to assist."

Headquarters came back with a response that the message had been received.

"They'll never reach us in time. Trace is almost here. There's nothing we can do to help." As the agent spoke, a small, slender branch flew off the tree and struck Red Beard in the back.

"There's something I can do, but keep your eyes open. Make sure they don't have an AMR to shoot at us!"

TJ pushed the control stick, and the helicopter dipped down. Red Beard didn't ease up or move away. Agent Belter leaned back and pushed his feet into the front of the helicopter like he was stepping on brakes that weren't there. He yelled something. TJ ignored him as the helo dipped lower. It was a game of chicken as TJ pointed the nose of the helo down and Red Beard aimed up.

Her family was in danger. She wasn't going to back down.

Tanya Stowe is a Christian fiction author with an unexpected edge. She is married to the love of her life, her high school sweetheart. They have four children and twenty-one grandchildren, a true adventure. She fills her books with the unusual—mysteries and exotic travel, even a murder or two. No matter where Tanya takes you—on a trip to foreign lands or a suspenseful journey packed with danger—be prepared for the extraordinary.

Books by Tanya Stowe

Love Inspired Suspense

Visit the Author Profile page at LoveInspired.com.

ESCAPE ROUTE

TANYA STOWE

LOVE INSPIRED SUSPENSE
INSPIRATIONAL ROMANCE

LOVE INSPIRED® SUSPENSE
INSPIRATIONAL ROMANCE

Recycling programs for this product may not exist in your area.

ISBN-13: 978-1-335-58725-1

Escape Route

Copyright © 2022 by Tanya Stowe

For questions and comments about the quality of this book, please contact us at CustomerService@Harlequin.com.

Love Inspired
22 Adelaide St. West, 41st Floor
Toronto, Ontario M5H 4E3, Canada
www.LoveInspired.com

Printed in U.S.A.

And almost all things are by the law purged with blood;
and without shedding of blood is no remission.
—*Hebrews* 9:22

For William Hewes and Les Featherstone.
Thanks for the inspiration to fly
and the expertise to make it sound a little bit right.

ONE

TJ Baskins pushed the control stick, and the helicopter dipped closer to the ground. She was careful to keep the copter tilted so the movement of the rotors would not wash away the tracks below. She'd been working for the border patrol as a contract pilot for almost two years now. She flew over the vast Texas borderlands near her hometown of Leytonville, looking for signs of foot traffic, men hiding in the bushes or concealed caches of drugs. This stretch of border was closest to the highway, and drug smugglers often hid their supplies under mesquite bushes or trees until their partners picked up the caches for the next leg of the journey.

Today, however, TJ was looking for signs of a different kind. Heavy vehicle tracks had crossed and recrossed the desert landscape. The two border agents on the ground confirmed the tracks were either a Jeep or a small pickup truck, not an all-terrain vehicle. That meant the loads they carried were very large. It was unusual for a heavy load to be crossing here. Usually, the packages were small enough for one man to carry across. If six wrapped packages of drugs were worth a million dollars in the States, the loads didn't need to be big. So what made this shipment different?

For almost two hours now, TJ had been following tracks that led nowhere or vanished. The smugglers obviously knew they were being tracked. That was why they spent so much time creating false trails that led into the desert. She was getting tired and feeling like she was wasting her time, but she hated to give up. The two men on the ground were good officers. She'd worked with Jefferson and Donetti before. They were some of the best at cutting sign—finding the hidden paths and tracks of smugglers. Jefferson and Donetti were experienced, smart and conscientious. She hated not being able to turn up something for them.

As another trail led to the highway with no sign of tracks or a hiding place, she circled back and radioed the men.

"No signs, guys. I've got one more path to follow. It cut off from the one headed south, so I took the trail closer to the main road. Maybe the southbound trail will point us to some action."

"Roger that." Donetti's deep voice echoed over the radio. "We're at the crossroad now. We're finding some promising signs here. Be careful, Baskins."

Donetti always signed off like that. He worried over her like a big brother. It was another reason she liked working with the duo. They cared. Genuinely cared.

Her altitude was low enough to see Jefferson wave as she passed over, headed south. It was dusk. They'd been at this all afternoon. Now if any action took place, it would be later. She wouldn't fly in the dark, so she wouldn't be part of that effort. Her work would end after this run, and she'd head back to her airfield. She hoped she could help the guys before she was forced to leave.

She came across a long stretch of dirt and noticed something different about the vehicle tracks. They were darker, maybe deeper. Like the vehicle carried something really heavy. TJ lightened up on the copter pedals and dipped lower for a better view. Up ahead was a grouping of mesquite trees surrounded by shorter bushes…a perfect place to hide a vehicle.

Suddenly, a squawk came over the radio. It sounded like a shout and maybe gunfire, but it was cut off so abruptly, TJ couldn't tell for sure. She pressed the radio button on her headphones.

"Say again, Donetti. I missed that."

Silence.

"Jefferson? Everything okay down there?"

More silence. TJ pulled her foot completely off the helicopter pedals and hovered just short of the brushy oasis.

She tried the radio again. No answer. Something was definitely wrong. She needed to go back and check on the officers. Just as she started to turn, a man stepped out from the mesquite bushes below. He was blond with a long braided ponytail hanging down his back. He wore jeans, a black T-shirt with a leather vest and patches. That all registered in a nanosecond… along with the fact that on his shoulder rested the stock of a rifle. TJ came from a military family. She knew the look of an anti-material rifle—a rifle designed to destroy vehicles. One was pointed right at her.

TJ hit the pedals to ascend. She was low to the ground. Moving too far to the left might cause her rotors to hit something. All she could do was hope her R-22 would rise faster than normal. It was a small helicopter created more for training and small trips, not for sharp maneuvers. But it was sturdy. She worked on it herself and kept it in tip-top shape…she hoped.

"Come on, come on," she whispered. The copter rose but not as fast as she would've liked, especially when she saw the AMR buck on the shoulder of the man below. She couldn't see or hear the round, but she knew it was coming.

"Please, Lord, let me get out of here."

The bullet didn't hit her. She continued her ascent. Suddenly she remembered something her grandfather had told her. As a Vietnam helicopter pilot, he fought many battles. He told her the mistake most pilots made was forgetting to zip-zag.

Move!

Clamping down on her panic, TJ shifted the control stick to the other side. The R-22 tilted a little more sharply than she liked, but it was just in time. She saw the rifle buck on the man's shoulder again. The bullet must have zinged past because nothing happened.

She kept the controls of the helicopter rising, praying every inch of the way, and weaving back and forth as much as she dared. Then she spun and headed back toward the agents. As soon as she was clear of the shooter on the ground, she punched the radio button on her headset.

"Mayday! Mayday! Shots fired."

A controller came on the radio and gave her call sign. "We've got you, Baskins. Give us your coordinates."

She radioed them back. "Some crazy man has an AMR. He's got heavy weapons. I can't reach Donetti and Jefferson on the radio, but I'm headed their way."

She came over a slight rise and found the two men. Jefferson was faceup, blood pooling in the white sand around him. Donetti was a few feet away, facedown. Neither man was moving.

"Oh, no." The words came out muffled as hot tears flowed down her cheeks.

"Baskins…do you have a visual?"

She couldn't speak, couldn't force the words through numb lips.

"Baskins…do you have a visual?"

"Yes, yes. Agents down. I…I think they're dead. I need to help them. I…"

"Get out of there, Baskins. Get yourself clear. Reinforcements are on the way."

TJ couldn't speak. Couldn't respond.

"Baskins, do you copy? Get out of there now. Do you copy?"

She swallowed hard and answered. "Yes, yes, I copy."

Trace Leyton eyed the border-patrol commander briefing him. Standing beside his commander was a

DEA agent and an FBI agent. The three agencies were working together, sending him on a special assignment for a big operation. He understood that fact, but it still made no sense to him. He was a border-patrol launch operator. He patrolled the reservoir named Lake Amistad, Spanish for *peace*, that spanned the US border with Mexico. Management of the lake was a joint operation shared by both countries, and he knew his patrol well. He was good, but not so good they'd pull him off to monitor an airfield…a type of operation he had zero experience with.

He knew the order was coming from higher up, and he was pretty sure his dad had something to do with it.

Trace took a slow, measured breath, trying to control his temper. Leytons had settled the area almost two hundred years ago. Their cattle ranch was the biggest operation in this part of Texas, and their family name carried a lot of weight. It was true his dad was less involved since his stroke put him in a wheelchair, but he still had a lot of influence. Trace's older brother, Chad, had a growing reputation as well. But Trace had walked away from the family legacy five years ago and joined the border patrol at an entry level. His father never understood why Trace refused his help, and ignoring his wishes, his father had tried multiple times to intercede "on Trace's behalf." But Trace didn't need or want that kind of help, and this seemed like another one of those "efforts."

The commander finished his explanation of how Trace would work undercover, ostensibly taking a leave of absence from his position at Lake Amistad. The commander explained how the department would like him to set up his travel trailer on the property of TJ Baskins.

"You are familiar with the Baskins and their airfield, correct, Officer Leyton?"

"Yes, sir. I know them. I went to school with Mike Baskins's granddaughter. I also helped him restore the aircraft on his field. But I'm a launch operator. What do I know about doing undercover work or performing babysitting duties?"

His commander was a little taken aback by his question and hesitated. "You were chosen, Officer Leyton, because you know the area and your family..." The man stumbled over his words. Apparently, he knew the weight the Leyton name carried in this part of the state, and it clearly caused him to walk on eggshells.

Special Agent Mike Gomez from the FBI had no such compunctions. He gave the commander a sharp look before stepping closer. "Here's what information we have, Officer Leyton. Over the past three months, several major robberies have taken place at selected weapon manufacturing facilities. They've stolen heavy arms such as automatic guns, Uzis and AMRs."

"Like the weapon that was fired at Miss Baskins's helicopter."

Agent Gomez nodded. "Are you familiar with the term the Iron Pipeline?"

"Yes, it's the term to describe the various routes from Florida to New York used by arms smugglers to get weapons in or out of the country."

"Exactly. After the robberies we cracked down on

the pipeline, made it almost impossible to get this large shipment out of the country. So the gang went deep underground. We thought we lost them until an informant told us about rumors of a partnership between two gangs, one running drugs from Mexico. When the smugglers made the mistake of using an AMR to fire at TJ, we knew we had our culprits and their alternative route."

"You believe the gang is using one of our smuggler's routes to get the arms out of the country."

Agent Gomez nodded. "We have TJ and Mrs. Baskins here in town. TJ is looking through our files, trying to put a name to the man she saw as well as the weapon. If she can identify those, we'll have the confirmation we need and we can safely send her home. Still, we'd like you to stay at her place to keep an eye on things."

"I still don't understand why me? If she needs a babysitter, I'm the least qualified."

Agent Gomez sent another glare in the commander's direction. "Ms. Baskins really doesn't need a babysitter. Once she identifies the man and the weapon and we can connect them to the stolen arms, she'll be out of imminent danger."

"You sound pretty confident you will connect them."

Agent Gomez nodded, and the look on his face grew hard. "I'm sure we will. I know these are our guys, but that's not the real reason we're recruiting you. When was the last time you had contact with Bill Denby?"

Trace eased back in his chair. Now his presence here was starting to make sense. Growing up, Bill Denby was his brother's best friend. Denby and Chad had raised Cain from here to San Antonio. After his dad's stroke, Chad had put his "bad boy" days behind him and taken over the management of the ranch. The last Trace had heard of Denby, he'd gotten involved with an outlaw motorcycle gang.

"I saw him ten years ago at my high school graduation. He blew into town on his bike, got drunk and ruined my graduation party. I haven't seen him since."

"What about your brother?"

Trace tensed. That was the question he'd been dreading. "My brother and I are not very close, Agent Gomez."

Why did he feel the need to preface his answer that way? Chad was a changed man. He'd pulled the ranch out of debt and turned it back into a profitable undertaking. His dad thought the sun rose and set on Chad now. So why did Trace hesitate?

Was it lingering emotions from the years of bullying he'd suffered from Bill and his brother? The threats to man up? The practical jokes to humiliate him because he was the popular captain of the football team dating a high school cheerleader? He never understood Bill's resentment, and he probably would have suffered worse treatment if Chad hadn't pulled back from doing any actual harm. Still…the feelings lingered, even though Chad had become a model son and businessman. He was even considering running for office in local politics.

Trace shook his head. "As far as I know, Chad hasn't spoken to Bill since that day either."

"As far as you know?" Gomez's gaze narrowed.

"I told you. My brother and I are not close."

"Because you live far away? If you were closer to home, say living at the Baskinses' airfield, you'd be able to determine if Bill Denby was in contact with your brother."

A cold feeling washed over Trace. "You want me to spy on my brother?"

Gomez smiled. "No, Officer Leyton. We want you to spy on your entire hometown…and while you're at it, keep an eye on an old friend."

The acerbic twist in Gomez's tone made Trace laugh. The man understood the irony of what he was asking, and he had a sense of humor. Trace liked that.

"On your duty tour tonight, you'll sustain an injury. Nothing serious. Just enough to put you out of commission for a few weeks and cause you to take your choice of work into consideration."

Someone had done their research and knew his family history. Trace gave a shake of his head. "That rumor should make my dad happy."

"Happy enough to welcome you back with open arms. At least, that's our hope. Let us know if Denby contacts your brother. In addition, small towns thrive on the kind of cover we've provided for you. We're hoping you can use that rumor mill. Put your ear to the ground. Listen to the whispers and give us a heads-up on any changes. We understand Denby still has a sister in town."

Missy had suffered beneath Bill's and Chad's tormenting as much as he had…maybe more. At one time,

Missy had feelings for Chad. But that relationship had ended abruptly, and Trace always wondered why.

As much as he hated to admit it, maybe this assignment was the opportunity he needed to resolve the issues of his past. It would give him the chance to spend time with his family. Maybe he'd find the answers he needed once and for all and settle some old hurts. It might be just what he needed.

The door opened. Another agent escorted TJ Baskins into the room.

Speaking of old hurts, Trace had some bad behavior he needed to own up to. He just hoped TJ would give him the chance to make up for the past.

Agent Gomez rose to his feet and gestured to Trace.

"Ms. Baskins, I think you know Officer Leyton."

TJ turned. Her lips parted in shock and her face paled.

Trace inwardly groaned. Obviously, she was not pleased to see him. Given her reaction, he might not get the opportunity to apologize. Taking the bit by the teeth, he nodded in her direction.

"Hello, Tara Jean."

Tara Jean.

Only three people called her that. Her grandfather, her mother and Trace Leyton. Everyone else gave in to her demand to call her TJ. But Trace, like her mother, had always claimed her name was too pretty to shorten and refused to call her by anything but that.

Against her will, hearing her full name in those familiar low tones made her stomach flip-flop. After all these years, her high school crush still had the power to make her feel like an awkward, bumbling teenager with grease under her fingernails.

That feeling was humiliating, and shock quickly turned to anger. She'd heard Trace had become a border-patrol agent, but he was stationed halfway across Val Verde County at Lake Amistad. Surely he wasn't the agent they were assigning to watch over her?

They wouldn't do that to her.

But there he stood, looking as handsome as ever in a green uniform with patches and a name tag. He'd removed his cap. His brown hair still swept to the side with those gold highlights all the high school girls admired. He was clean-shaven to suit the uniform code, and the slight cleft in his chin added a rugged look to his too pretty features.

His eyes were just as dark as ever, hooded so you could never really tell what he was thinking—if he was making fun of you or just being silent while others did it. They'd become friends the first summer he helped her grandfather work on his derelict planes. But when they'd gone back to school and the popular kids in his crowd made fun of her, Trace had stayed silent.

That was what she remembered most. Did he remember too?

His eyes hadn't changed. She couldn't read them, hidden as they were by his brow.

She wanted to turn and walk out. Wanted to say she wouldn't agree to this.

But that would put out a signal that what lay between them still mattered. And she wouldn't let that happen. Wouldn't let the past swallow her up again. She'd worked too hard to climb out of that hole, and she refused to go back.

Taking a deep breath, she nodded. "Hello, Trace. So you're the one they're putting on my property."

"If that's all right with you."

"It doesn't look like I have a choice."

"Yeah…me neither."

She should have known Trace might get involved when she came across an FBI photo of Bill Denby. She'd heard that he'd become involved in an outlaw motorcycle gang. It didn't surprise her. Denby was trouble as a teen. No one knew that better than TJ. She had been one of Denby's favorite targets. At times, Trace had been the recipient of Denby's cruelty, too. Just remembering the man sent a shiver through her.

It seemed God had a sense of humor. He was determined to make her face all the problems of her past, even the ones she'd tried so hard to keep buried.

"We're working on getting your paperwork set up, Officer Leyton. It should be ready for pickup day after tomorrow. That will give you forty-eight hours to pay a visit to the hospital where a medical order will be waiting for you. Then you'll load up your trailer. You do have a truck to haul it, correct?"

His question made TJ smile. Trace was born on a Texas ranch. Of course he had a truck. The same thought must have struck him because he had a wry tilt to his lips as he met TJ's gaze.

It seemed some things never changed. She and Trace still had the same brand of humor. In fact, they'd had a lot in common back in the day. Too bad Trace hadn't had the good sense—or the courage—to admit it.

"Yes, I'll handle it."

Gomez nodded. "Good. We'll make sure your leave is cleared by your superior and the scuttlebutt will take care of the rest. We'll keep Ms. Baskins busy for at least another day. She'll be returning home the same day as you."

Surprise swept over TJ. "I'll be here another day? Your agent said I'd gone through all the photos."

Gomez smiled. "Oh, you're done with the people. Now we want you to identify the rifle. If we can connect what you saw with some of the missing weapons, that'll build my case. So far, we've been able to keep your name out of the news. We'd like to keep it that way. The fact that you're a contractor has helped tremendously."

"I still have to work. I have some contract jobs. I'm spraying a field day after tomorrow."

Gomez nodded. "Keep to your normal activities as much as possible. If the gang doesn't know about you, maintaining your usual routine will keep their suspicions down. After that, we have another job for you. We'd like you to scout out the county north of the border and pinpoint any facilities where the gang could hide their weapons cache. That'll keep you busy, and a long way from the scene of the crime."

TJ nodded. Fly over the county and find large storage facilities. She could do that. It would be easy.

"I have one more piece of information for you both.

This shooting was the first big mistake this gang has made, and it gave us our only lead."

"Mistake? You mean because I can identify the shooter?"

Gomez shook his head. "Partly, yes. But also because this morning, Mexican authorities found a body in the desert just over the border. The body matches the description of your shooter, TJ. If you can positively identify him in our records, we'll send dental records down for verification. But we're pretty sure he's one of Denby's men. His body was found in an area known to be a dumping ground for a particular gang."

Trace jerked in reaction. "Wait a minute… You think Denby's gang is working with Los Desaparecidos?"

Gomez nodded and Trace released his breath. "That's not good."

TJ shook her head. "I don't understand. Who are they and what does their 'dumping ground' mean?"

Trace turned to her. "We don't know much about Los Desaparecidos. No one is willing to testify or give out info about them because they keep very tight reins on their members. Anyone informing or making mistakes ends up dead in the same area of the desert. That way everyone knows Los Desaparecidos were responsible. It keeps their members in line and everyone else, too."

She inhaled sharply and turned to Gomez. "You think Denby murdered his own gang member?"

"He probably had to," Gomez said. Los Desaparecidos don't tolerate mistakes. They wouldn't allow anyone to expose the gang and stay on board. If Denby wanted to continue his partnership with them, he probably had to kill his man."

TJ fell back against her chair.

Gomez went on. "Most likely Los Desaparecidos won't take any more chances. They'll stay on their side of the border. There'll be no more pickups on this side, and that will force Denby and his crew to move the weapons to them. To do that, Denby will need local help, someone in the area."

Trace visibly tensed. "That's why you think Chad is working with him."

Gomez held up his hands in a placating manner. "I'm not convinced it's your brother. We've done our research, and like you said, your brother's record is exemplary. But Denby needs a large storage facility, and there's plenty of those on the Leyton ranch."

Trace shook his head. "There's a large barn or silo on just about every ranch in the area."

"Exactly. That's why we need you to connect with your family. Talk to your brother. Find out if he's involved or if he's aware of any unusual activity in the area. We may even need you to contact Denby's sister, Missy."

Trace released a heavy sigh. TJ felt every inch of his frustration. Dredging up the past was their only recourse, and it made her just as uncomfortable as it seemed to make Trace.

Gomez gathered his files and stacked them on the table. "Any other questions?"

TJ and Trace exchanged a glance before shaking their heads in the negative.

"Good. I'll leave you two to settle the details. Officer, you'll need to get back to your post for tonight's shift. I want everything to go as planned."

Gomez nodded in TJ's direction, then headed out the door. An awkward silence followed his departure.

Trace broke it. "I was sorry to hear about your grandfather's passing, Tara Jean. He was a good man."

TJ caught her breath. "You must be one of the few people in town who thought so."

Her grandfather's drinking had been the source of much of TJ's humiliation in her youth.

Trace's features hardened. "That's not true. Anybody with any sense knew your grandpa was a hero."

"Vietnam was a long time ago, and people's memories are short."

Eager to forestall any more discussion about her grandfather, and especially about her dad, she changed the subject.

"It surprised me to hear that you and Chelley broke off your engagement."

A snort of laughter broke out of Trace, almost as if he couldn't contain it. He shook his head. "Why would you be surprised by anything Chelley did? She treated you like trash."

Trace was acknowledging Chelley's bad behavior toward TJ? Would wonders never cease? She didn't know what to say, how to respond, and another awkward silence grew between them.

Trace ducked his head. "Sorry. I shouldn't have said that. I can't blame anyone else for the past. My mistakes are mine, and for those I'm truly sorry, Tara Jean.

You were a good friend, and I should have treated you that way. If you can't forgive me, I understand. But I needed to say that."

Now TJ was completely flummoxed. She stared at Trace, trying to read his true feelings. All she saw was open honesty in his brown-eyed gaze. The silence stretched on.

At last, he said, "Will you accept my apology?"

She licked dry lips and tried to gather her thoughts. "Of course...of course I do."

He gave her a nod and a brief smile. "Thanks. I've waited a long time to say that."

Her lips parted again. Trace had waited a long time to apologize? She couldn't believe it...and if he kept surprising her like this, the next few weeks were going to be strange, maybe even difficult. The last thing she needed was more difficulty.

Maybe this whole thing was a mistake. Maybe she should talk to Agent Gomez...

Trace rose and grabbed his cap from the table. "I'm assuming I'll park the trailer near your grandad's workshop where I can connect to the power?"

She nodded, still unable to formulate words or follow his brisk changes in conversation.

"Great. I'll be there day after tomorrow. I'm looking forward to seeing your mom again."

With that, he fitted his cap onto his head, nodded again and headed out the door.

TJ stood in silent amazement as it closed behind him.

But why was she so surprised? Of course Trace

would apologize. He was the town's original Boy Scout and everyone's favorite. He would be the first to apologize and admit his mistakes. The first to try to do right…and he'd be the first to fail. His intense optimism always blinded him to the truth. As a kid, he'd refused to believe his brother could do such awful things. He wouldn't stand against his brother in his own defense, let alone hers. She would never trust Trace to do what was right again…no matter how many times he apologized.

Trace's optimism and loyalty would never allow him to tell the truth about his brother. Gomez didn't realize it, but he'd just set his mission up to fail. For the sake of her friends Jefferson and Donetti, TJ was going to do everything in her power to see that that didn't happen.

TWO

TJ pulled the control bar of the Piper back slightly. She made a circle around the field, then headed back the way she'd come. "Now watch, Squirt. It's important that you stay level as you sweep the field."

Squirt was a fourteen-year-old boy from the local foster program. He'd been with her all summer long, working on the planes for her grandfather's museum. The youngster was brilliant, hardworking and passionate about flying. He'd volunteered to set up a computer spreadsheet to log the changes and improvements they'd made on the aircraft. He'd even offered to research each of the planes' convoluted flight histories. If anyone could do it, it was this bright young man with blond hair that stood straight up in an uncontrollable cowlick and vivid blue eyes that were hidden behind bottle-thick glasses.

Squirt was having a lot of trouble with his foster mother. So when he asked if TJ would teach him to fly, she couldn't say no. Of course, she couldn't give him flying lessons, but she'd agreed to take him along on several jobs and show him the ropes, maybe even familiarize him with the controls and approaches. He had loved their outings and was a quick learner and so determined to fly, she had no doubts that someday he would make an excellent pilot. However, he was going to be very unhappy when she told him their extra time in the air had to end. Today was their last day. She couldn't risk having Squirt, or any of the foster children she worked with, on the airstrip with Denby cruising the area.

She leveled the wings and came in for an approach on the field she had been crop-dusting. "Now, watch this. It's important to stay level for an even disbursement. Do you see that knob, the yellow one?"

The boy nodded so vigorously, his glasses slid down on his nose and he had to shove them up quickly.

"All right, I want you to pull it out."

"Do it fast or slow?"

"Slow and only go a quarter of the way. We have four more passes to make before we finish this field."

With his tongue sticking out a corner of his mouth, Squirt pulled the knob exactly as TJ had instructed him. She smiled. The boy was a natural. Hopefully he could maintain a good relationship with his foster mother long enough to finish out the summer. But that might not happen. Squirt had already discussed how unhappy she was with him. Today was no exception. She didn't like him asking to be driven all the way out to the airfield for extra training.

TJ made another wide loop and came back, swooping down as Squirt pulled the knob a little farther out and grinned like he'd just won a marathon. TJ smiled too. Teaching him about flying was a delight.

They made two more sweeps over the field. On the last one, she stayed low to the ground and crossed over the dry river gully that marked the edge of her employer's field. She'd passed over it many times today, but now she was low enough that something caught her eye. Deep tread marks wove down the center of the dry wash. Smaller tread marks crisscrossed back and forth, resembling the ATV tires that marked every trail, gully or dry wash in the area. But the deeper treads were exactly like the ones she'd seen near the border. Was it possible Denby was using this wash to transport his weapons away from the border to the north of the county?

She glanced at her watch. The rest of the foster children wouldn't be coming to the airfield for another hour. She and Squirt had just enough time to follow the tracks to see where they went.

"We're going to take a little jaunt up the dry riverbed, Squirt. How would you like that?"

"Awesome!"

Of course he would enjoy this new adventure. He had expressed an interest in working for the border patrol or some other form of law enforcement. This was an opportunity to show him what it was like.

TJ wasn't sure his foster mother would approve of the opportunity, but she didn't approve of anything Squirt wanted or needed. Plus, Gomez had told TJ to stay far away from the border. She intended to follow his instructions. She would just follow the tracks north and never go south.

She banked the Piper right and flew above the wash. She felt a momentary stab of guilt about stretching Gomez's boundaries. But right now, she was his best hope of finding Denby's gang. She had little confidence in Trace. He'd moved away from Leytonville almost four years ago. Lots of things happened in a small town in that time. She wasn't certain Trace would still have the contacts he needed to get info from the townspeople. Plus she wasn't certain he would get any useful information from his brother.

Based on her experience, Trace had taken his brother's side many times in the past, so he might do it again. It was true Chad had been a model citizen for the last five years, but where Denby was concerned, TJ didn't trust anyone or anything. He was volatile and dangerous, and one of his gang members had murdered two of her friends and colleagues. She was going to make sure Denby and his men were stopped.

She circled back over the wash just in time to do a little more teaching. "Look down there, Squirt. Tell me what you see."

"Uhhhhh. Lots of ATV tracks. Maybe some side-by-side tracks too."

TJ nodded. "Good. Take a closer look and tell me what's different about those tracks."

"Well…wait. There are some really big ones that go right up the middle. They're really dark."

"Why are they dark?"

He leaned close to the window, looking down, and

squinted. "I think, yeah, they're deeper than the others."

"Why would they be deeper?" She knew she was reaching. For any other teen, it might be a stretch. But Squirt was exceptionally bright, and she wanted to challenge him with her question.

"Because the vehicle is heavier?"

TJ grinned. Reaching over, she patted his shoulder. "That's exactly right. Someday you're going to make a great pilot for the border patrol."

The boy beamed as if she'd given him a new car. "So where do these tracks go? And who would be crazy enough to drive a heavy vehicle down the middle of a sandy wash? Aren't they afraid of getting stuck?"

TJ's jaw tightened. "Well, I guess that's what we're going to find out."

She dipped the control handles down and leveled off to a height just above the trees that ran along the gully. Cottonwoods, mesquite and brush lined the dry wash. The trees thrived on the underground water, just beneath the surface. The county hadn't had rain in several weeks and it was a good thing for whoever was driving up the gully. Otherwise, they would have been bogged down in mud just beneath the thin layer of dry dirt. That made TJ think that whoever was traversing the gully knew the area well. Denby fit that bill.

With grim determination, TJ guided the Piper along the wash. But soon the steep dried embankment wall gave way and crumbled down, forming a perfect driveway out of the gully. All the vehicle tracks went up onto the hard-packed earth above. TJ tried to follow along, but the tracks soon disappeared.

"I can't see them. Where did they go?" Squirt leaned forward until his nose and eyeglass frames pressed against the window.

"The tracks are there. We just won't be able to see them from the air. Our work here is done."

"But where did they come from? Can we go figure that out?"

TJ smiled. Yes, Squirt was going to make a fine law-enforcement officer someday. He had a logical, inquisitive mind. But he had a lot of things stacked against him, starting with his poor relationship with his foster mother. Many kids who left the foster care program with pristine records often had difficulties fitting into law enforcement. One like Squirt, with a record of problems with his foster mother, would have a hard time finding work in the border patrol. It would be a tough road for him. Left with that unhappy thought, TJ ignored Gomez's warnings and Squirt's foster mother's possible concerns to give him one more unplanned little adventure. She turned south to check out the source of the tracks.

They flew back the way they had come and crossed the field they had just dusted. The wash wove back and forth, twisting and turning, eating up what was left of TJ's fuel. She stopped following the gully and cut across the distance to a large cluster of trees and bush, very near the border. The white bark of a cypress grove stood out against the dark leaves of the water-loving cottonwoods. Neither tree was native to the area, probably brought in by a long-ago Spanish cattle drive. Squirt asked her about the unusual trees. She'd begun to explain when a bright flash of metal caught her gaze. She paused, uncertain she'd seen it. Then it flashed again.

"Did you see that?" Squirt asked. "It looks like there's a truck or something inside those trees."

Squirt's comment confirmed TJ's fears. A part of her wanted to fly closer and see if someone was hiding in the copse of trees, but the image of the AMR bucking against the shoulder of her assailant flashed in her mind. No way would she let that happen with Squirt on the plane. Sweeping to the left, she headed back home.

"Wait… We're not going to check it out?"

She didn't want to alarm Squirt, so she shook her head. "I'm running low on fuel. We need to head back, but I'll call and have someone check out that metal flashing in the sun. It's probably just some debris that washed down the gully in the last rain."

It sounded good, but Squirt stared at her, not blinking or turning. Like everyone else who lived on the border, he was aware of the illegal traffic that went back and forth across it. Ignoring his pointed stare, she contacted the Del Rio BPS headquarters.

A controller came on the line. "I have a possible vehicle or metal debris near the border." She gave them her plane's numbers and her name, then said, "I think we need a team to check it out."

She winced slightly. Now Gomez would know she'd disobeyed his instructions. But it was better to be discovered than to let Denby escape. She gave the controller the coordinates, then clicked off.

She'd have to deal with Gomez later. Right now, it was time to get Squirt out of harm's way. But all the way back, she caught him sending her speculative glances. She hadn't fooled him with her report of metal debris. But she said no more. The less said to Squirt and his inquisitive mind, the better.

Trace pulled his truck to a stop on the hilltop overlooking the Baskinses' airfield. The place looked much the same, only neater. It appeared that Tara Jean had been very busy since her grandfather's passing and had gained much headway in creating the air museum that had been his dream. Over the years Mike Baskins had assembled quite a collection of damaged and abandoned planes, which he hoped to restore. He had acquired civilian planes such as a 1965 Piper Twin Comanche, two smaller firefighting craft and a Beechcraft air tanker. He'd also gotten his hands on military planes, a 1951 Bell helicopter used during the Korean War and a Cobra—the same type of helicopter he'd flown during his Vietnam War years. But his prize had been a 1943 Kittyhawk from World War II.

Trace always thought the reverence Mike attached to each plane's service was because of the lack of reverence he received when he returned from war. Thankfully, when his only son's jet had gone down in Iraq and he was killed, Captain Justin Baskins had received a hero's honor.

Mike Baskins had given many of Leytonville's trou-

bled teens a place to be and something of value to do.
Mike had chosen Trace to be one of his Misfits, the
name he gave to his band of workers. Trace was certain if he hadn't spent that summer and several after
working at the airstrip, he would have had run-ins with
the law and his border-patrol career would have been
over before it began.

Tara Jean walked out of the rounded Quonset hut
Mike had purchased from a military sale. A small
group of teens trailed after her. So—she had continued her grandfather's custom of inviting troubled teens
to work during the summer. He smiled. It pleased him
to know that. But he shouldn't have been surprised. It
was just like her. Underneath that stubborn exterior
was a very soft heart.

He shifted his truck back into gear and headed down
the hill. The heavy trailer behind him kicked up enough
dust on the road to catch the attention of the group
below. He waved as he looped out onto the airstrip,
turned around and pulled to a stop beside the hut. He
exited his truck and walked toward them. As soon as
he was close, one very young-looking teen with short
blond hair and thick glasses turned to face him.

"Were you shot in the line of duty?" His squeaky
voice testified to his young age.

Tara Jean grimaced and put a gentle arm around
the youth's shoulders. "Squirt, that's not a very polite
thing to ask before you've even been introduced." She
met Trace's gaze. "I told them you were injured in the
line of duty and would be staying here a few weeks
to recover."

The youngster ducked his head, but it popped up quickly and he held out his hand. "Hello, Mr. Leyton. Were you shot?"

A few of the older teens laughed, and Tara Jean rolled her eyes.

Trace shook the young man's slender hand. "Squirt is a very...unusual name."

The teen shrugged one shoulder. "It fits. I don't look my age."

Trace suppressed a chuckle. "Well, if you're okay with it, I guess I am too. The answer is no. I wasn't shot. I pilot a launch. I hit some rough waters and fell. I have a head injury, which means I can't be on duty."

"TJ says you used to work here too. Is that why she doesn't need us for the next few weeks? Because you'll be doing all the work?"

This time Trace didn't even try to stop his chuckle. Squirt obviously had a very active mind. "No...umm. Tara Jean has a very special project she'll be working on for the next few weeks. I'll just be recuperating."

He sent a questioning glance in her direction, hoping his story worked for her. She nodded, but Squirt wasn't convinced. His glance shot back and forth between Trace and Tara Jean. Trace swore he could see the youngster's thoughts racing back and forth as well.

Not a moment too soon, a small van pulled up. A county logo on the side identified it as an official vehicle. Tara Jean said her goodbyes to the young people, and they headed toward the van. Squirt dragged his feet and continued to look back. Doubt riddled his features. He was the last to board.

"I don't think he believes our story," Trace said in a low voice.

Tara Jean agreed. "Squirt is one of the brightest kids I've ever worked with. It's hard to pull the wool over his eyes. He's in the foster program, like the rest of them. But Squirt's very attached to me and Mom... and he's very protective."

Trace nodded slowly. "I can understand that. You know just how to handle kids like him."

She gave him a level look he couldn't read. "I should be. I've been a misfit all my life."

That was true enough. Trace often wondered what it must have been like for Tara Jean growing up without her father. His relationship with his own father had been so fraught with tension he sometimes thought it would have been easier to be fatherless. But he knew that wasn't true. Tara Jean always seemed like she didn't know where she belonged. She'd been a shy, gawky child and looked even more out of place as a teenager.

But then Tara Jean took ownership of her reputation and defied popular opinion. She dyed her spiky hair blue and her fingernails black, long before that color was an accepted style. Trace always admired her spunky defiance. Looking back on those times now, he wished he'd been half as brave. It would have saved him a lot of heartache.

There was nothing awkward about Tara Jean now. She'd always been tall and skinny, but softer curves mellowed her bony angles. She still wore her black hair short, but the spikes were gone, and her long bangs were swept to the side with a gentle wave. Large silver hoops adorned her ears. She must not have done any work with the teens today because she wasn't wearing her overalls. Instead, she wore jean capris and a loose V-neck sweater that fell off one shoulder very attractively. In fact, everything about Tara Jean was attractive. She seemed comfortable in her skin—her lovely skin.

She pointed to his truck and trailer and turned to look at him, catching him looking at her shoulder. He jerked his gaze away.

"That plug on the side of the workshop is fifty amp. It will take care of everything in your trailer."

Flustered at being caught staring, Trace ducked his head. "Good. I'm going to need my air-conditioning. I've gotten used to the cooler air coming off Lake Amistad."

He walked toward the trailer, purposely keeping his gaze on the ground. Pulling the long black cord loose from his trailer, he plugged it into the outlet beside the hut.

"Trace Leyton! Come here and give me a hug!"

Eva Baskins, Tara Jean's mother, walked toward them. She looked much the same except that her long, sixties-style hair had gone completely white. It hung well below her shoulders and framed her face like a silvery veil. She had a few more wrinkles around her mouth and eyes. Laugh lines. He was sure of it because Eva was all light and joy. Her free spirit and steadfast faith had carried her family and had lightened Trace's path as well.

She grabbed him in a fierce hug, and he returned her embrace.

"I am so glad to see you!" She pushed him to arm's length to study his face. "I hear you joined the border patrol. What a wonderful decision. I'm so proud of you!"

Trace smiled with an inner glow. It was good to know someone was proud. Even his own mother had expressed displeasure at his decision. Trace pulled her back in for another hug.

"It's real good to see you too, ma'am. You don't know how good."

She cupped his face and smiled. "I reckon I might have a good idea." Her tone said it all. No words were needed.

She released his arms and gripped his hand. "Come on up to the house. I've got some sweet tea ready and I want to hear all about it."

"Actually, ma'am, I'm headed back into town. I have some work to do."

"All right, then." She patted Trace's arm. "But you will join us for dinner. It's not much. Just a big pot of pinto beans with cornbread and fried potatoes. But as I recall, those are some of your favorites."

"Yes, ma'am. They are, but I'd appreciate any of your good home cooking."

Trace walked toward his truck and TJ followed. He glanced down at her attire.

"I didn't think you were going to work today. You're not dressed for it."

"I've got to make sure the planes are tied down.

Mom says there's a storm front headed our way. Looks to be a doozy."

Trace smiled. "Your mom is still the airfield's weather reporter."

Tara Jean flashed a quick smile in response. "Still. And she's much better at it than I am."

She moved toward the Piper, parked close to his trailer.

Trace pointed to the tanks on the side of the aircraft. "Those look brand-new."

"They are. I fabricated them myself two weeks ago."

"Still doing all your own welding in the shop." He nodded as he glanced back at the rounded hut. "I wouldn't mind getting my hands dirty. What are you working on now?"

"A gyrocopter."

"Sounds like it could be a handful in these Texas winds."

She sent a mischievous grin in his direction. "That's what makes it fun."

"I think I'll stick to the bigger craft. Thank you very much."

She laughed. "Says the man headed into town to confront criminals."

"No criminals. I'm just checking in with some of my BPS friends. See if there's any talk about Denby's gang."

"Good idea. See you tonight." She waved and continued onto the airstrip.

Trace unhooked the trailer, settled it in place, then drove into town. His first goal was to scout out Missy

Koslowski's place. Denby's sister had a small two-bedroom place close to downtown that she'd inherited from the uncle who raised her and Bill. She'd returned with her infant son to take possession of her uncle's house after a short-lived disastrous marriage to a man who never showed any interest in their son.

In high school, Missy and Chad were a couple, but Chad's continuing involvement with her brother and his troubles caused a rift. At least, that was what Trace suspected, but Chad would never admit it. In fact, his brother never spoke of Missy at all, but Trace knew he secretly kept tabs on her and her boy.

Missy's small house was old, but the yard was neat as a pin. A couple of rosebushes flourished near the porch. He slowed his truck to take note of the license plate on her car. As he did so, the front door opened. Missy's young son ran out and jumped down the steps, headed toward their parked car. Missy followed him, her purse on her shoulder and an orange-colored apron draped over her arm. Orange was the color of the HiLo Supermarket where she worked. She was probably headed in for her shift. Missy glanced up, saw Trace's truck and froze.

Caught in the act of spying, Trace slowed even more and gave her a casual wave. She didn't wave back. Sighing, Trace continued on his way. Whatever had happened between Missy and Chad still clouded her relationship with Trace. Or maybe she knew her brother was back in town and rightfully suspected Trace was a border-patrol officer checking out her place. Whatever the reason, Missy wasn't happy to see him.

He continued along the street to the downtown area and parked near Leytonville's old-fashioned town square. A call to some local law-enforcement friends gave him a tip. A local mechanic by the name of Jose Martinez was rumored to service vehicles for Los Desaparecidos. No one had tried to prove it, but the shop did a lot of high-volume business.

Trace stepped outside his vehicle, pulled the cap off one of his tires and let out some air, just enough to make the tire low. Then he drove to the Martinez Auto Shop. His contacts were right. It was a busy place. Customers waited inside and out. Vehicles filled the parking lot outside and the shop lifts inside the large garage doors.

The man at the front desk had a name tag that said Martinez. Trace nodded. "You the Martinez on the sign outside?"

"That's me. Aren't you Trace Leyton?"

It was hard to get away from his family's name. "Yeah, that's me."

"Leytons don't usually come to this part of town."

Trace tensed. "My money is as green as everyone else's."

Martinez smiled but it wasn't pleasant. "Word is, Leyton money is greener."

Trace took a slow breath. "Can you look at my tire or not?"

Martinez dropped his pen on the counter. "Sure. I'll take some of that green Leyton money. But it'll be a while. We're busy."

Trace looked around. "I'm in no rush."

The man nodded again. "Good."

He sauntered toward the garage, leaving Trace wondering if he'd made a mistake. He waited outside by his truck, casually observing the men who came and went, but he didn't recognize any faces.

A while later a serviceman took his truck inside the shop, raised it on a lift, removed the tire and checked for leaks. It only took minutes, and Trace was impressed with the efficiency of the Martinez team. Definitely professional enough to service a big drug operation, and well worth watching.

While his vehicle was still on the ramp, Martinez sauntered out of the office toward him. He carried a clipboard in his hand. "Hey, Leyton."

The man's call was casual enough, but the hard look in his gaze didn't match his tone.

"You work for the border patrol, right?" Now the hard glint in the man's eyes matched his tone.

Trace nodded.

The man returned the nod. "I thought so."

With that, he walked to the man working on Trace's truck and said a few words. The man dipped his head in agreement, then followed the manager back to the office. The tire was back on Trace's truck. The work was complete, but his truck stayed on the ramp for another ten minutes. Then fifteen.

Workers buzzed around the vehicle beside his, brought it down from the ramp and brought another one in. Trace watched in silence. Almost thirty minutes had passed since his talk with the manager. Trace was getting nervous.

Then, slowly but surely, all the workers drifted inside the shop. Activity slowed to a crawl. Only customers were left outside. A few of them started to complain and look around. One headed to the shop door and opened it. A worker spoke to him. The customer shut the door, hurried to his car and drove away. Other customers got nervous. They kept watching Trace and glancing back at the closed door of the shop. Some left. Even so, the parking lot was still full of customers. If the men in the shop intended to start something, a lot of people could get hurt.

Trace studied the men in the office through the glass window. By his estimate the count was ten men. Ten against one. Not great odds…and his service weapon was in his trailer. He was supposed to be on the injured list and not carrying. He gritted his teeth and made up his mind to take his small .22 out of his gun safe. It was small enough to tuck in his boot. But right now, he was a sitting duck. He pulled out his phone. He was ready to punch in Gomez's number when the workers filed out of the office and started back to work.

Trace heaved a sigh of relief, but still the man working on his truck didn't come out. He waited another fifteen minutes before he exited, lowered the ramp and backed Trace's truck out into the lot.

Moments later the manager came out of the office and once again sauntered toward him.

"All done, Mr. Leyton. No leak and no charge."

Trace shook his head ruefully. "Thanks."

"No problem. Come back any time." The sarcasm in his tone matched the glint in his eyes.

"Right," Trace drawled. "I'll be sure to do that since you made me feel so welcome." With that, he marched toward his vehicle. But he didn't release the breath he'd been holding until he was safely inside the cab of his truck and the engine was running.

THREE

Trace headed straight to the border-patrol office and related his encounter with Jose Martinez and his men at the car repair shop to Agent Gomez. The agent agreed that they needed a surveillance team for the place. Trace also updated the agent on Missy's not-so-friendly reception.

"But her reasons could be personal. I honestly don't believe Missy would have anything to do with her brother. At least, the girl I knew wouldn't."

Gomez shook his head. "That could be true. Still, we need to keep tabs on her. But not you. I don't want you to go by there again. You'll just arouse suspicion. We'll do it." The agent sighed. "I'm running out of manpower, but we'll do the best we can."

"Can't you put in a request for more help?"

Gomez grimaced. "My superiors think I'm heading down a false trail, but everything in me says I'm on the right one."

"It might not count for much, but I agree. The men at the Martinez shop were super protective. They could have simply serviced my car and sent me on my way. But they took pains to warn me off." He shook his head. "The whole parking lot was full of innocent bystanders. An altercation would have been bad for everyone. It was a bold move."

"Everything about this operation has been bold and in our face. For the life of me, I can't figure out why Denby would take the chances he has."

"You don't know Denby. If you did, nothing would surprise you."

"I'm beginning to think you're right." He handed Trace a sheaf of papers. "Here's a contract for Ms. Baskins. I went ahead and gave her the regular BPS payment for hours in the air. I think that's only fair."

"She's worth it. She's the best pilot I know."

"Well, I need you to keep a good eye on things."

"Don't worry. The tire incident put all my senses on alert."

"Good, you're going to need them. TJ decided to disregard my directions and took a plane down by the border."

Trace paused. "What?"

"Apparently, she was up in the air with one of the foster kids she works with, and they spotted tracks in a nearby wash. Ignoring my directions, she followed the tracks to the border. At least she turned away before she got too close. Good thing too. The vehicles had cleared out, but my team found evidence of heavy vehicles and motorcycles."

"You think it was Denby?"

"I believe so."

Trace released a sigh. "Tara Jean could have been shot at again."

"And what's more, I'm sure they can identify her now. How many local pilots fly a Piper and a helicopter?"

Gomez gestured to the contract. "I'm not sure I should have created that. It might have been safer not to involve her at all."

Trace shook his head. "Trust me, it's safer to have Tara Jean involved. If you didn't, she'd just take off on her own, and you'd have no way of knowing what she's up to. At least this way, you'll have some sort of clue as to what she's doing."

"Has she always been this…"

"Stubborn. Independent. Willful—"

Gomez raised a hand. "I think I get the idea."

Trace smiled. "She takes after her granddaddy and her father. Both of them were veterans and men of action."

Gomez shrugged. "Well, let's just hope we can keep her a little farther away from the fighting."

Trace smiled. "We can try."

Gomez laughed and waved goodbye.

All the way back to the airstrip, Gomez's words filtered through Trace's mind. He didn't like the idea that Gomez's team was shorthanded. He wondered if he might be able to call on some friends to help. But Leytonville was such a small town. Word traveled fast, and Denby still knew people here. Trace couldn't take the chance of word getting back to him that they were aware of his plans and beefing up their support. Better to keep things on the quiet side…at least, for the time being.

The afternoon's events had unsettled him. He would be glad to put it all behind him and hunker down for the night. He parked by his trailer. Even from the distance he could smell good food in the air. He washed his hands and hurried up to the house for dinner.

"About time you showed up. This peach pie was going to go to waste." A twinkle in Eva's eye made the teasing even more pleasing than the mention of his favorite pie.

They enjoyed a pleasant meal. As they were finishing up the dishes, Eva looked out the window.

"I don't like the looks of those clouds, Tara Jean. You best go close the hut. That lightning and wind are about to hit."

"I have to tie the gyro down, too. I forgot to do that this afternoon. I'll have to push it close to the Piper to get it secure."

"I'll help." Trace tossed the dish towel he'd been using to dry the dishes onto the counter and hurried after her. The wind was already tossing Eva's rosebushes in front of the house back and forth. Rose petals flittered through the air. A glance behind the house told Trace that her garden was going to take a beating too. Her tomato plants were bending over double.

As Tara Jean hurried forward, the phone rang. Eva's soft tones echoed as the door closed behind them. Tara Jean shoved the large doors of the hut closed while Trace pushed the lightweight gyro toward the Piper. They'd have to use the same concrete block to secure the gyro. By the time they finished, the black clouds were above them. There was no rain yet, but it was coming.

Eva ran toward them, her long white hair flying around her head.

"That was Mrs. Fisk, Squirt's foster mom!" she shouted over the rumbling thunder. "She says Squirt has run away again."

Tara Jean sagged. "How long ago did he go missing?"

"About two hours. He was supposed to be at a karate lesson, but he never showed up. She didn't find out till she went to pick him up. She's fit to be tied and says she's done. She won't take him back when we find him. She's already called his social worker to come and get his things."

Trace frowned. "Two hours is a long time to be missing. You'd think she'd be a little more concerned about him being out in this storm than getting hold of the social worker."

Eva pulled her long hair out of her face. "I guess that explains why he goes missing so often, don't it?" Her worried frown added to her words.

"Two hours is enough time for him to walk out here." Tara Jean cinched the gyrocopter's strap into place. "He's not hiding in the shop, but he could be in one of the planes. I'll start looking." She headed to the closest plane.

"I'll start at the other end." Trace crossed the airstrip as the wind whipped up. Jagged lightning lit the sky. If that youngster was stuck out on the open road somewhere, the risk of getting struck by those bolts was doubled. That thought made Trace speed up his steps.

He climbed into the first plane and looked down its empty cargo shaft. The boy was nowhere in sight. He hurried down the ladder. A glance across the airstrip showed Tara Jean and Eva making headway through the other aircraft.

He checked the next plane and found nothing. As he headed to the large cargo plane at the end of the strip, the boy ran out the back and headed up the rise of the nearby hill.

"Squirt!" Trace shouted the boy's name, but the wind picked up his voice and threw it back at him. The youngster continued to run. Trace couldn't let him get away. He charged toward the hill, running as fast as he could against the wind. Squirt was a good fifty feet ahead of him. If Trace didn't pick up his pace, he'd never catch him. But running up the slope against the strong wind slowed him down. Trace gasped for breath and his thighs were on fire.

Suddenly, Squirt reached the top of the hill and stopped. He wasn't running away from Trace. He was running toward something!

Trace came up beside the youngster, puffing and panting. He still had to shout against the wind and booming thunder. "Squirt! What are you doing?"

He pointed down the other side of the hill to a clump of trees. "Two men. They were watching the house with binoculars. I saw them from the plane. When y'all came out to close everything up, they turned and ran down the hill."

Shocked, Trace studied the clump of trees. It was large enough to hide two motorcycles. Large enough to even hide a car, and the clump was next to the road leading into town. If Squirt had truly seen the men, then Gomez's fear that Denby's men had identified Tara Jean was true.

Trace squinted against the wind, looking for any sign of movement. The trees bent and the branches whipped in the wind, but there was no sign of activity.

"That's why you're here, isn't it? TJ and Miss Eva are in danger, aren't they?"

Trace looked down at the young teen. There wasn't any point in hiding the truth from him. "Yes, I'm here to keep an eye on things."

Squirt nodded. "I knew it." He nodded again. "That's it, then. I'm not going back. You can't make me."

Trace didn't have the heart to tell the youngster he wasn't welcome back even if he decided to go. That was information for Tara Jean or Eva to relate.

"We'll worry about that later. Right now, Tara Jean and Miss Eva are out here looking for you, and they're worried sick. We need to get them inside out of this storm."

The young boy ducked his head. "I'm sorry. I didn't mean for them to worry. I just knew they were in danger."

Trace sighed. Lightning lit up the sky. "Get on down there and let the ladies know you're all right."

He pointed Squirt down the hill. He heard Tara Jean shout over the wind, and the boy ran down the hill into

Eva's arms. A few drops of rain sprinkled over them all. They bundled him toward the house. But Trace turned and walked a few feet down the other side of the hill. The ground on this side was softer with lots of loose soil—soil that might show him some footprints.

He walked farther down, and sure enough, he found two pairs of boot prints heading down the hill toward the trees, just as Squirt had said. It was possible the intruders came up the road, parked their motorcycles in the trees and hiked up the hill to spy on Tara Jean. Denby's gang had identified her. But even if they did know, they also had to assume she'd already identified the shooter and the gun. Like Gomez said, she should not be in imminent danger. But the men were here. What did they want?

A low rumble echoed in the air. Trace couldn't tell if it was motorcycle engines or distant thunder. The storm was all around them now. Lightning flashed too close for comfort, and thunder boomed directly overhead, drowning out every sound.

If those men were members of Denby's gang, they were caught out in this storm. They were going to have to ride through muddy patches, slick roads and wicked lightning strikes back to their base, wherever it was. The ride would be difficult and dangerous.

Trace hoped so.

Just as that thought came to him, rain dropped from the sky like from a bucket. He was soaked to the skin in seconds.

He smiled. "Welcome to west Texas, boys."

* * *

Eva hung up the phone and nodded to Trace and Squirt. Tara Jean was on the airfield, checking for damage after last night's hailstorm. Their county didn't get many tornados, but the hail was always vicious and damaging. Last night had been no exception.

The older lady looked at Squirt. "Your social worker just gave us the okay to keep you with us until another more permanent placement can be found. I just have to go into town and sign some papers."

The look on Squirt's face seemed to ask the same question in Trace's mind. *Why can't he stay forever?*

If Trace was in the youngster's position, he would want to stay with Eva and Tara Jean. It would have been a dream come true for Trace, and he had a family. He could only imagine how badly Squirt might want to stay with the two women. Eva seemed to sense the question, too.

Wrapping her arms around the boy, she said, "Let's just take things one day at a time, okay?"

Squirt nodded, and Trace agreed with the sentiment. Even so, the situation ignited a longing inside him he couldn't define. Was it a need to belong? To help? He couldn't pin it down, so he didn't try. Right now, with the gang members scouting the property, this was the last place the youngster needed to be. That was an undeniable fact.

"I've alerted Agent Gomez about our intruders. He said if Tara Jean checks in by phone, it should be safe enough for you to go into town without me. He wants me to pay a visit to my family."

It was something he couldn't afford to put off any longer. Besides, the men invading the airstrip yesterday had started an idea percolating in his mind. He was eager to follow up on it…even if it meant confronting his family and their issues.

Tara Jean returned to report no damage to the airfield or the planes, so they loaded into their trucks. Trace followed them down the road until they reached the turnoff to his family's ranch. He called Tara Jean on her cell and told her to be careful.

"You too," she replied. "And Trace, I'll be praying for you."

That was all she said. A few simple words, but they told him she understood the depth of his unease for the task ahead of him. That thought filled him with the courage he needed.

"Lord, I know this is what you want me to do. Help me do it right." He shifted into gear and headed down the road.

The sprawling ranch house had two wings stretching out on each side of the large entrance. It was a six-bedroom house, meant for entertaining. Trace remembered the days when state and federal officials had visited the ranch for his parents' lavish parties. But those days were long gone.

Trace could see ranch hands working near the barn on the rise just beyond the house. These were busy days, and Trace hoped that meant his brother, Chad, was out in the field. It would be easier to confront one Leyton family member at a time.

He parked under the large portico and headed for

the front door. Before he touched the handle, it opened wide. Betty, the Leytons' housekeeper, stood with one hand on the door and another on her hip.

"It's about time you showed up. Your dad's been in a fever ever since he heard about your accident."

Betty and her husband, Sal, had worked for the Leyton family for as long as Trace could remember. They were more like family, though he doubted his dad would admit it. He gave Betty a kiss on the cheek.

"Kissing me isn't gonna ease my irritation with you. Listening to him fuss for the last two days has made my work tougher than usual."

"I'm sorry, Betty. That's about the only reason I would've come home sooner."

She patted his arm as she shut the door. "Well, no matter. Your dad doesn't need much of a reason to get flustered these days. He's in his office with Chad."

"What about Mom? Where is she?"

"On her way home. She was working at an orphanage in Honduras. But your father called her and told her you were hurt. Sal is picking her up from the airport now."

Trace groaned. "I told him it was nothing to worry about."

"I know that, and so does your mother. But he uses any excuse to get her home."

"I should have called her to let her know I was all right."

Betty shook her head. "It wouldn't do no good. Your mother uses any excuse to come home and check on your dad, too."

She was probably right. His parents' dysfunctional marriage was one of the things he tried to avoid. He hated being the reason for them to play games with each other.

"Go on." Betty pushed him toward the office. "No use putting it off any longer."

She was right. He headed down the hall toward his father's office where he heard his father and brother discussing something in a slightly heated tone.

Great. Just what he needed to walk in on. A brewing argument. When he entered the office, his father was seated in his wheelchair behind the massive mahogany desk. His brother was standing off to the side. Chad looked almost relieved to see him—or, at least, relieved to break off the conversation with Dad.

"Well, look who finally decided to pay us a visit." An amused smile played about Chad's lips. "Where you been hiding yourself, brother?"

Trace tried to avoid a direct answer. "I told Dad I was okay. I haven't had a vacation since I started, so now seemed the right time for one."

"You live in a trailer on the edge of Lake Amistad. Every day of your life is a vacation."

Was that a hint of envy he heard in Chad's voice? His brother had never expressed a desire to do anything besides run the ranch. Where was this resentful tone coming from?

Chad and his father stared at him expectantly. There was no getting around it now. He had to reveal his location. "I pulled my trailer over to the Baskinses' airfield. I enjoyed my summers there. Working on the airplanes is relaxing, and that's what I need right now."

Both men stared at him like he was crazy. Thankfully, a commotion at the front door forestalled their comments. His mother breezed in on a perfumed gust of air. She grabbed Trace in a fierce hug, then held him at arm's length.

She nodded firmly. "I figured you weren't hurt bad, but I wanted to see for myself."

Crossing the room, she gave Chad a similar hug before turning her gaze on her husband. "You look worse than the two of them put together."

"Well, what do you expect since I'm the only one here watching over our sons?"

"Our sons are adults. They don't need watching."

And so the arguments started. It would go on from here. Trace caught Chad's gaze and nodded toward the door before stepping out. Chad followed. Neither of their parents noticed. As soon as they reached the living room, Trace turned to face his brother.

"I need to ask you something. When was the last time you saw Bill Denby?"

Chad took a step back. "I haven't seen you in over a month, and that's the first thing you ask me?"

"I'm sorry, Chad, but Denby's in serious trouble. Just before I left the office, I saw an APB. He's wanted by the FBI."

Chad frowned and looked away. "I haven't heard from Bill in years."

That little glance away made Trace uncomfortable. He decided to approach his brother from another direction. "What about Missy? Have you talked to her lately? I know you try to keep tabs on her."

Chad glared at him. "Why shouldn't I keep tabs on her? Her deadbeat husband left her with an infant son to support. I'd help her more if she'd let me."

"I'm not questioning your concern for Missy, Chad. I agree completely. But that's why I'm worried. If the FBI is after Bill, the last thing she needs is him showing up at her place."

Chad shifted his shoulders. "Bill's trouble no matter who's looking for him."

Trace released a breath he didn't even realize he was holding. He was glad to hear his brother's confirmation of what he knew to be true. It eased his suspicions about his sibling.

"If he shows up, let me know. It's my duty to tell my superiors."

His brother nodded. "Sure. Of course I will."

But he wouldn't meet Trace's gaze, which made Trace's confidence in his brother's sincerity waver. But before he could question Chad more, his phone rang.

Tara Jean's shaky voice echoed over the phone. "Trace, we stopped for groceries before heading home. A man on a motorcycle followed us out of the parking lot. Then on the highway, two more pulled out behind him. Those two are speeding up, trying to get in front. I don't know what to do."

Two motorcyclists sat on the side of the road up ahead of TJ. They kicked their bikes into motion, preparing to pull out in front of her. They were going to box her in.

"Tara Jean..." her mother began.

"I see them, Mom."

She handed her phone to her mom. She could barely hear Trace's voice. "Turn your truck around. Head back to town. Go to the grocery store parking lot and wait there. They won't try anything with witnesses around. I'll be there as soon as I can. And, Tara Jean, don't get out of the truck."

There was no room on the road ahead to turn around. Besides, if she stopped to do that, the men behind would catch up. They might have guns and could force them out of the vehicle. No, it was safest to keep moving.

But if they thought she would balk at running over them, they were wrong. She would do whatever necessary to protect her mom and Squirt. Thankfully, just ahead was a dirt path. A barbed-wire fence blocked access to the path, but her truck could easily go through it.

"Hold on!"

Her mother's arm automatically shot across Squirt's body to protect him. He was buckled in between them on the truck's bench seat, but it gave TJ an added reassurance to know Mom was just as protective of him as she.

TJ slammed on the brakes. The truck screeched to a halt. One cyclist behind her almost rammed into the back of the truck. He avoided it only by shooting off the road into some mesquite bushes. TJ turned to the left. The truck shot across the lanes onto the opposite shoulder. She hit the accelerator, and the vehicle shot through the barbed-wire gate and sped down the road, kicking up a dust cloud behind her. Dragging the wire fence behind her, she spun the truck in a circle and shot back onto the road.

The motorcyclists who had been following her were now in front of her. The barbed-wire gate bounced behind her and swung wide. The bikers struggled to get out of the way of the swinging gate. It struck one biker, snagged him and snapped the gate loose from her truck. The biker went down and skidded across the blacktop.

TJ didn't slow. She barreled through the remaining bikers. It didn't take them long to regain their momentum. In her rearview mirror, she saw them pausing momentarily and turning one by one to follow her. There were only five of them. The sixth must have damaged his bike in his trip across the asphalt because he didn't join them.

She tried to remember if one of the five bikers looked like Bill Denby. Years of his torment kept his image burned into her mind. She was pretty sure he wasn't one of them. Still, she studied them in the mirror, trying to memorize any significant features. If she got out of this, she wanted to be able to identify them for the FBI. If they got out…

The bikers headed toward her truck with just as much purpose as TJ felt. They were gaining on her. She had five more miles to go before reaching the outskirts of town. Her truck was older and built for hauling, not for speed.

Suddenly, one biker pulled up from the rear and passed his partners. He had black dirt streaks down one side of his body, and dust covered his shiny bike. Most likely he was the one who went off the road. He seemed more determined than the others to exact some sort of retribution because he shot ahead of them, bending over his bike handles, pushing for extra speed.

If he got in front of her, he would try to box her in again. She wouldn't let that happen. She gripped the wheel tighter, mentally preparing herself to do damage if necessary. She pushed the accelerator down, but it was already floored. Her poor old truck had no more speed to give.

TJ gritted her teeth. No way would she let the motorcyclist get in front of her. Mom had been looking behind them. Now she turned around, and her arm shielded Squirt again. She knew what was coming.

TJ saw yellow lights flashing in the oncoming traffic. Was it a state trooper? Could she flag him down?

She waited a moment more, just long enough to determine that the flashing lights belonged to a lead truck warning motorists of a wide load coming on the two-lane highway. If TJ could just make it to the caravan, the bikers could not get past her, and she would reach the town's outskirts safely. Hopefully Trace was right, and the bikers wouldn't do anything once they had witnesses.

The lead biker saw the caravan too and leaned even lower on the handlebars. He pulled out onto the oncoming lane of traffic to pass TJ. His bike reached the back edge of her truck and inched forward. TJ gripped the wheel, prepared to bang into him if necessary. No way would she let him get in front.

The driver of the oncoming truck honked. Once. Twice. The biker didn't slow down. He inched closer to TJ's truck. He was almost at her door.

The truck with the flashing lights laid on the horn. The blast roared across TJ's nerves. She wanted to ram into the biker and end the tension. Yet she clung to the wheel, hoping he would ease off.

But he didn't stop. He was going to run into the truck!

At the last second, he slammed on the brakes. His front wheel wobbled so much, TJ thought he might lose control. If he crashed now, this bike would tumble into TJ's truck. She might not be able to maintain control and would ram into the large load coming toward them.

But the man kept his bike upright and pulled into the lane right behind TJ.

It took a few moments for him to pick up his speed again. TJ used the time to put distance between them. She didn't ease up on her speed until she hit traffic near the center of town. Then she slowed and let out the breath she'd been holding for miles.

Thankfully, she didn't hit any stoplights and pulled into the busy parking lot of the HiLo Supermarket. As she turned off the ignition, she heard her mother release her breath in a long sigh. Squirt shifted in his seat and stared up at her, his eyes as wide as fifty-cent pieces.

TJ let go of the steering wheel. Her fingers were

cramped from gripping it so tightly. She started to relax, but the rumble of motorcycles made her tense again. All six motorcyclists pulled into the parking lot and stopped near the driveway in an open space. The lead motorcyclist, the one who had almost passed TJ, kicked his stand down, slung his leg over the tank and marched toward their truck, his red-bearded features set in a fierce rage.

"Mom, lock your door." TJ's tone was low.

She heard her mother's lock click and quickly pushed hers down, never taking her gaze off the furious man striding toward them.

Trace had said to stay in the truck until help arrived. But he hadn't planned on a biker determined to punish her. Should she start the engine and drive away? What if he had a weapon?

He put a hand behind his back. He did have a gun. TJ reached for the ignition.

A shout echoed to their left. TJ looked up to see Missy Koslowski. Her orange HiLo apron strings flapped in the wind as she marched toward the man. The biker hesitated. Missy came closer, and this time, TJ heard her shouted words.

"I said leave them alone!"

Still, the biker hesitated. His partners yelled something TJ couldn't make out over the rumble of their engines. The man cursed and spun away, running toward his bike. In seconds, the men had turned around and sped out of the parking lot with the angry biker trailing the pack.

TJ flung her door open and ran to Missy. She

grabbed her old schoolmate in a fierce hug. "That was the bravest thing I've ever seen."

Missy laughed. "Not so brave. They belong to my brother's gang. They've been riding up and down my street for two months now, trying to scare me, but they've never harmed me. I'm pretty sure Bill told them not to hurt me, although for the life of me, I don't know why."

Trace sped into the parking lot with his truck. He flew out of the cab and charged toward them, halting only when it registered that Missy was standing beside TJ.

"Missy…"

"Hey, Trace." She gave a quick shake of her head. "When I saw you drive down my street, I knew something was going on."

At that moment, four FBI vehicles zoomed into the parking lot and surrounded them. Missy, TJ and Trace stared in slightly stunned silence as agents piled out of the vehicles and ran toward them.

Trace nodded slowly. "Yeah, you could say something is going on."

Relieved laughter slipped out of TJ. "The understatement of the year."

Squirt ran out of the truck and hurried up to Trace. "You should have seen it!" He pointed to Missy. "She scared a crazy biker and made him run away, and TJ outran a whole crew of them! It was awesome!"

Trace ruffled the youngster's spiky hair. "I can't wait to hear all about it, Squirt. Sounds like we've got some pretty amazing women on our hands." He spoke to the boy, but his gaze was on TJ—and the look in his eyes took her breath away.

But the last thing she needed right now was that same, unwanted reaction she always had to Trace. She pushed the breathless feeling aside to concentrate on the question at the back of her mind.

She had linked the AMR used to shoot at her helicopter to the same kind that had been stolen. She had identified the man who had shot at her as one of Denby's men. But he was missing, or dead if his body turned out to be the one in the Los Desaparecidos' dumping ground. They still had no proof linking Denby to the crimes.

She was a witness to the attempt on her life, nothing more, and Gomez already had her written statement. He said she would be safe after that.

So why were Denby's men risking their freedom and their safety to get at her?

FOUR

Trace's cell phone buzzed with a message. He, Missy, Eva and TJ were inside the local border-patrol office. Missy was relating how Bill had shown up out of the blue, declaring he wanted to meet his nephew. Missy knew he was up to no good and had ordered him to leave. She knew less about Bill's plans than the rest of them. When Gomez apprised her of her brother's criminal activities, the look on her face signaled her distress.

"Murder and robbery." She shook her head. "I can't be involved in this. My son…"

Before their meeting, she had called Bobby's sitter and told them agents were on their way to pick him up and bring him to the office. Trace saw Squirt's concerned features and was amazed when the youngster's protective nature came out. He immediately introduced himself to Bobby and suggested they play video games in the other room. Trace was thankful for his quick thinking, but the action also indicated that Squirt had been at the police station before and knew about the video games in the room. Not a good thing.

Gomez reassured Missy. "We're aware of your need to protect your son. That's why we would like to bring you both into protective custody."

"Protective—wait. I have to work. I can't just disappear. I'll lose my job."

"I'm certain your supervisor would prefer not to have a repeat of today's incident in the parking lot. That couldn't have been good for business. He'll see reason."

"So Bobby and I will just...leave our home?"

Agent Gomez nodded. "Temporarily. Until we can find your brother. The alternative is to deal with him on your own."

"Maybe that wouldn't be so bad. Neither he nor his men have harmed us."

"Do you think that's because of brotherly affection or some other reason?"

Her expression fell. "If I know Bill, he has some other reason. Bobby and I are just pawns in whatever game he's playing."

Gomez's tone changed. "Do you have any idea what game that might be, Missy?"

She closed her eyes and ducked her head. She was silent for a long while. At last, she said, "I've never been able to figure out my brother, Agent Gomez. I stopped trying a long time ago."

Trace's phone buzzed with a message. It was from his mother. She was giving him the okay for the women and children to stay at the ranch. He had proposed the idea to Gomez, and they had been waiting for a confirmation from his mother.

"But where will we go? I can't afford..."

"Don't worry, Missy." Gomez paused and looked at Trace, who gave a nod.

Gomez continued. "We've arranged for you and the Baskinses to stay at the Leyton ranch."

"What?" Tara Jean and Missy spoke at the same time.

Trace was taken aback by both women's vehement response. Tara Jean was the first to argue.

"We can't do that."

Trace shrugged. "Why not? Our property is isolated. We have enough ranch hands to watch the grounds. If the bikers approach from any direction, we'll know instantly. The house has plenty of rooms. It's the perfect solution. Especially since we've determined that you have a target on your back. Apparently Denby's gang blames you for the loss of their member."

"I didn't kill him."

"Tell that to the man in the parking lot who charged your truck…with your mother and Squirt inside, I might add."

Tara Jean hesitated and glanced at Agent Gomez. "I…I have to work. I'm scouting out the area north of the border for you. I'll need my airstrip."

"You know as well as I do the ranch has plenty of places where you can take off and land."

She didn't have a response to that, but Missy stepped in with her own protests.

"I'm not comfortable with this. That's far too much disruption in my son's life. I'm not leaving just because you're worried something might happen."

Gomez raised his hands and shook his head. "I can't

force you. You're not in imminent danger—at least, not yet. But I want you to think about this. My men can't do the legwork involved in this case and protect your home and the Baskinses' airstrip at the same time. Having you all in one place is the best solution."

Missy shook her head. "Those men backed away from TJ on my command. I can't imagine they'd turn around and hurt me. Bobby and I will stay in our home."

Her tone indicated there would be no more discussion. It looked as if Tara Jean wanted to continue arguing, but her mother spoke.

"We already know our place isn't safe and Tara Jean is a target. We appreciate your mother's offer, Trace. We'll be happy to stay someplace with better protection. We can count on the Leyton ranch hands to keep an eye on us."

Her daughter didn't seem so happy, but she stopped protesting.

Trace lifted his phone. "If you'll excuse me, I'll speak with my mom and let her know to prepare for our arrival."

He headed for the door. Tara Jean rose and followed him. As soon as they stepped into the hall, she closed the door. "Trace, listen to me."

She dropped her tone as a clerk passed them. "I didn't want to say anything in front of Gomez, but I think this is a bad idea."

Trace frowned. "What couldn't you say in front of Gomez?"

She folded her arms. "Come on, Trace. You know how close Bill and Chad were."

"Yes, Tara Jean. They were close when Chad was a rowdy teenager. I think ten years should be enough time to prove he's changed. Besides, I asked him point-blank if he's had contact with Bill. He said no."

"You believed him?"

Her question made him want to jump to his brother's defense. But he paused and reined in his irritation. He remembered the hint of resentment and envy in Chad's tone. Trace wasn't sure what had caused those emotions. He needed to find the source of those slight but disquieting remarks. But he also remembered the angry disgust in his brother's voice when he spoke about Denby.

"I believe he finished with Bill a long time ago."

"Well, I don't believe him."

Her tone—in fact, her whole belligerent attitude—shattered Trace's thin control. He couldn't hold back his defensive feelings any longer. "Back in the day, Chad and Bill made things difficult for you, but what has Chad done lately that has you so sure of his guilt?"

Tara Jean stepped back, surprised by his question. "Are you kidding? Forty minutes after you went to the ranch, six bikers came out of nowhere and followed me. Do you think it's a coincidence that they knew exactly where I was?"

Trace shook his head. "You know as well as I do they were already watching your property. They were probably spying on you the whole time you were in town, just waiting for the right time to grab you."

Her shoulders sagged, but she set her pert little chin in determination. "I still feel like they had help."

Anger flared to life inside him. "Well, it wasn't from Chad. I didn't tell him or anyone else at the ranch about your location or what you were doing this morning. No one in my family, especially my brother, knew you were involved until after the incident. The bikers had to find you by another source, not Chad. Besides, Gomez agrees with me."

He walked away, then turned back. "Instead of cross-examining me and my trust in Chad, maybe you'd better look at your own feelings and lack of trust."

He stalked away, still sensing the burn of her accusation. He gave his mother a quick call, then stepped out into the hot afternoon sun. The BPS office was a squat, long building surrounded by parking lot asphalt. Its acrid smell rose to meet him, and sweat immediately beaded on his forehead. He stalked away from the building to the shade of a tree near the sidewalk.

Why had Tara Jean's questions made him so angry? Was it because deep down, he secretly doubted Chad?

Once again, he slowed his thoughts and went over his conversations with his brother. The unexpected envy and resentment. The way he wouldn't meet his gaze. Those things made Trace second-guess Chad's denial of any info about Denby. The only reassuring fact was Chad's sincere dislike of Denby. Trace had no doubt about that.

But the other conflicting actions needed explanations. What bothered him most about Tara Jean's questions was the lingering resentment he sensed behind her words. True, Bill and Chad had been unkind, but that was ten years ago, more than enough time to forgive. How could she still have such a negative attitude toward Chad?

During Trace's summer working there, he'd gotten to know her well. He understood that she put her trust in few people, and his actions when they returned to school may have reinforced her inherent mistrust of people in general. Had those wounds gone so deep she'd lost the ability to trust anyone?

What was more, if she couldn't forgive Chad, could she really forgive Trace? Or was her acceptance of his apology just words?

All his life Tara Jean had been a shining example of a good Christian. Someone who was pure, simple and straightforward. Yes, she was opinionated, and she spoke her mind. But she'd never been unkind or wishy-washy. She'd been a constant source of goodness Trace could count on.

Right now, some of her luster had dimmed and that rocked his world.

Sweat tickled its way down the side of his face. He swiped it away and pounded the tree trunk.

This was not how things were supposed to go.

A slight breeze swept over him with a cool touch. He closed his eyes and let it soothe his heated brow... and his anger.

Maybe Tara Jean was right. Bringing her to the ranch might not be the best idea. In fact, if her suspicions were correct, Trace was playing right into

Denby's hand. Chad would know their every move and could feed Denby updated info.

On the other hand, with Chad and Tara Jean so close together, it would give Trace the perfect opportunity to watch them both. If he could stay on top of their movements, he could protect Tara Jean and prove his brother's innocent once and for all.

If he couldn't, then he would be setting Tara Jean up as bait and himself for a cataclysmic failure.

That put him between a rock and a hard place. But one thing he knew for certain: he had to move quickly. Denby had already murdered two border-patrol officers. He had to be stopped. Trace could do a better job of that surrounded by his family and ranch hands than he could at her airstrip.

Taking a deep breath, he marched back to the building.

TJ folded another shirt into her bag, then paused in her packing. She was almost done. All she needed now was her cosmetics. As it had so often, her gaze wandered out her bedroom window and down the slope to Trace's travel trailer. He was hitching it to the back of his truck in preparation for the move to his parents' property.

It was late in the day, but the high temperatures hadn't let up. Heat waves shimmered off the metal siding of the trailer. Trace paused and wiped his forearm across his forehead. It was a subconscious move, but suddenly, TJ found her mouth was dry.

Why did he still have the power to do that to her? Even when he was angry with her?

He hadn't spoken to her since they'd exchanged words in the hallway. He'd stalked out, leaving her speechless and in turmoil. His words had shaken her, but he'd spoken the truth. She had to admit she might be holding on to the hurt Chad had caused her.

She'd been examining those feelings all afternoon and come to one conclusion. She had harsh feelings toward Chad, not just because he was cruel, but also because Trace chose his brother over her.

That hurt more than anything—apparently, more than she'd realized. The fact that it was happening again, that Trace was so quick to defend his brother over her concerns, triggered her latent resentment.

She regretted her hasty response and wished she'd toned it down, but she couldn't shake the feeling that something was not right with Chad. Something didn't add up, and she couldn't put her finger on it.

Her mother knocked on her door, jerking TJ out of her thoughts. She quickly grabbed another shirt to fold into her bag. "Come in."

"I just got off the phone with Squirt's social worker. She can't find another placement for him right now. She'd have to move him out of the county, and she doesn't want to do that. She says he'd just try to run away again and she's right. He would. Since we're staying with the Leytons, she's giving us the okay to keep him…just until she can find another place in town. If we weren't going to the ranch, she said we would have to pack him up and bring him in right now."

TJ shoved the shirt in her bag. "Yet one more example of the Leytons' majestic power."

Her mother paused. "Stop that, Tara Jean. She's right…as was Agent Gomez. We'll be safer on the ranch. They can give us double the protection, so I can't understand why you object to going."

Her glance strayed to the window one more time. "I don't understand it either, Mom."

"Are you sure? It's obvious you and Trace had words."

"Yes, we argued about Chad. I don't trust him, and that made Trace angry. He said I was letting my resentment toward his brother cloud my judgment."

"Was he right?"

TJ flopped on the bed. "That's the part I'm not sure about. I do have some resentment toward Chad, but not for his bullying. It's more about how Trace sided with him and abandoned me." That was the horrible hurt that went deep. Too deep.

Her mother nodded. "And now you think it's happening again."

TJ inhaled. "I don't know. I think I jumped the gun with my accusations. I could have been more sensitive to Trace's feelings…and he was right. There was no way Chad could have known where we were. But I still have this gut feeling that something's not right."

Mom headed toward the door. "I'm the last person to tell you not to trust your instincts, but like your grandad, you can hold a grudge better than most. Still, you need to make it right with Trace. All this useless bickering isn't helping our situation. I'll pray for the

Lord to give you clarity. In the meantime, I'm going to take full advantage of the Leytons' reputation and hospitality. The last thing Squirt needs is another new foster home. He's better off with us."

That truth hit home with TJ. Squirt needed them right now. She'd been so caught up in her feelings for Trace that she'd lost sight of that. Maybe it was better she and Trace keep their distance. Then she could focus on what really mattered and not on the past or what she wished would happen in the future. She needed to put her emotions on the back burner and concentrate on finding Denby and his gang.

Either that or she needed to make peace. Because she doubted very seriously that she could put her emotions concerning Trace behind her. They'd seared too deep inside her. Still, she had to work out something… but it would be on her terms. Not Leyton ones.

With that decision made, she grabbed her cosmetics bag, stuffed it inside the case and zipped it closed. She joined her mother in the living room as she was latching windows and locking up the house.

"I'm going to close the workshop doors."

Squirt was sitting on the porch, grilling FBI agent Belter about his job. What kind of gun did he carry? Had he ever shot anyone?

TJ chuckled as his words echoed through the screen door.

Her mother laughed, too. "That boy has the busiest mind I've ever seen."

"He's a force to be reckoned with, that's for sure."

TJ hurried down the steps to the Quonset hut. She

pulled the doors shut, placed a chain through the lock and secured it. Then she hurried over to Trace's trailer.

"We're almost done. How are you doing?"

"I'm about finished too."

She hooked her fingertips into her back pocket, not sure where to begin. She asked the first thing that popped into her mind. "You never said why you changed your mind about law school and joined the border patrol instead."

"With everything that's going on, that's what's on your mind?"

"I've just been wondering. Your dad must not have been happy about your decision."

Trace's lips twisted into the one-sided smile TJ loved. When he gave his usual wry smile, one corner lifted more than the other. That smile defined Trace more than any other feature. It was the one TJ saw in her mind when she thought of him.

"That's an understatement. Dad had an apoplectic fit. Chad still blames me for causing Dad's stroke."

TJ shook her head. That was one more thing to blame on Trace's brother. "He knows better. Your dad had a habit of throwing fits. I'd say a lifetime with that kind of temper led to the stroke that put him in a wheelchair, not your decision."

Trace ducked his head. "Yeah, I expect you're right."

His one-sided smile popped up again. It tugged at TJ's heart. Not to mention she was a little surprised by his reaction. Could it be that Trace, the most popular kid in high school and the town darling, was insecure?

She thought she knew everything about him. But she'd never considered this.

"I'm not surprised by your dad's reaction," TJ went on. "What I want to know is what made you change your plans. What happened to you?"

"That's easy. I left home, and the first thing I learned was how little the Leyton name meant. Here everyone knows my family. Our name opens doors and makes waves. But at college, I was just another student. It suddenly struck me that I needed to mean something. I needed to matter, to be someone."

He met TJ's gaze. "I wanted to be the kind of man willing to serve others, not just Leyton interests. I wanted to be like your dad. I decided the best way I could serve was here in Texas, with the border patrol. So that's where I ended up."

TJ nodded slowly. "A life of service is not an easy one. Everyone you love serves, too. Even the youngest." She was thinking of Squirt.

Trace focused on TJ. His gaze was so full of concern, it did funny things to her insides.

"It's who your dad was. Who you are. You're not much different."

TJ glanced up. Trace was watching her, and the look in his eyes took her breath away. No one had ever looked at her with such admiration. Her heart skipped a beat and she had to turn away again.

An awkward moment followed as TJ struggled to ask her next question.

"So, what did happen between you and Chelley? You two dated all through high school."

Trace chuckled. "That again." He shook his head. "As soon as she found out I wasn't going to live at the grand old Leyton ranch or spend my life in Leytonville enjoying the benefits of my family's reputation, she left. Claimed she didn't know me anymore and scooted off to Dallas. I hear she's married to a lawyer now and is enjoying high society."

"Lord have mercy on those folks." TJ's soft murmur made Trace burst into laughter.

She half smiled and ducked her head. "What? There's no sense putting a fine shine on it. She had enough ambition to take on a town the size of Dallas. We all know it."

Trace shook his head. "I didn't. Not until she dumped me like a hot potato."

She searched his features. "Did she really hurt you?"

He thought for a moment, then looked her straight in the eye. "No, I think she did me a favor. I knew there was someone better for me. I just needed to be patient."

TJ's heart stopped beating. Was he trying to tell her she was that someone? Was that why he rushed to apologize in the first few moments they were together? She didn't know what to think or what to say. This conversation had taken such a quick turn, it flustered her.

She needed to get away before she got any deeper into emotional turmoil. "I...I'd better go check on Mom. She was almost ready when I left."

She scurried up the hill and never looked back. At the house, she grabbed her bag and her mom's and carried them to the porch just as Trace pulled up in his truck. Agent Gomez had sent Belter along to accompany TJ on her helicopter flight to the ranch. He didn't want her traveling alone today. Squirt and Eva would be riding with Trace in his truck.

Trace loaded all the bags into the bed of his truck, then looked at Squirt. "All set, buddy?"

The boy nodded vigorously and climbed in. Trace opened the passenger door for her mother. As he came around the front again, he gave TJ a curt nod and got in. She watched the dust settle as the truck climbed the hill overlooking their property. Then she turned to Agent Belter.

"Let's go."

The agent nodded. They crossed the airfield to her helicopter and she went through her normal flight check, which took a little more time than usual.

At last, she put her headphones on and gestured for the agent to put his on as well. Then she flipped on the engine and took off. Rising above the airfield, she felt a tinge of regret. She hated leaving everything— her whole life—behind. But she thought of Squirt and knew she had to move forward.

They flew over Trace's truck just as he turned onto the main highway. Squirt leaned out of the back window and waved, his skinny arm seeming small against the landscape below. TJ smiled. They would arrive at the ranch long before Trace would. She scanned the countryside one more time before veering off. Bright metal flashed along the highway just as she turned.

"How long will it take us to reach the ranch?" Agent Belter's voice came over the headphones.

"About twenty minutes since we're traveling as the crow flies. It will take Trace about thirty minutes."

The agent nodded, and the noise of the helicopter took over. She flew over another hill. Metal flashed again along the road in the distance. A car was far ahead. The sight of it made something click in her mind.

The flash she'd seen just before leaving Trace had not been on the road. It had come from a grove of trees that marked the boundary of the abandoned Truesch farm.

"Wait a minute…"

"What's that? I didn't hear you." The agent turned to her.

"Did you see something in the grove of trees before we turned?"

Belter paused. "No, but my situational awareness doesn't usually extend to flight patterns. Did you see something?"

She glanced in his direction. "I thought so but I'm not sure."

The agent's features hardened before she heard his words over the microphone. "You've been cutting sign for the BPS. I trust your instincts. Turn back so we can check it out."

TJ nodded and gently tilted the helo's control stick to the right. They spun around and headed in the direction they'd just traveled.

"Does Trace have a radio in his truck? I want to give him a heads-up."

"I don't know. Call my mother."

She pulled her phone out of her pocket and handed it to the agent. "Her number is first on my speed dial."

While he dialed, TJ's mind churned. "If it is the gang, they'll try to box him in like they did me. He won't be able to maneuver his truck and turn around. He's towing that trailer."

The agent nodded in agreement before speaking to her mother. "Trace wants to know if you see another road he can turn onto?"

"Just a dirt one, and that'll reduce his maneuverability even more."

"He has to do something. He can't outrun them."

"We're almost back there. Let's see if it's them first."

There was less cover on the back side of the tree grove. Three or four bikes were parked behind the trees. Their shiny metal parts glistened in the sun. But did those bikes belong to the gang?

The helicopter came closer. Wind began to blow through the trees, whipping leaves and flinging branches. One man stepped out from the shelter. His red beard flashed bright.

It was the man who had come after her in the parking lot.

"It's them!" She punched the radio on her headphones. "Mayday! Mayday! Attack waiting for Officer Leyton at the Truesch farm. Attempting to assist."

Headquarters came back with a response that the message had been received.

"They'll never reach us in time. Trace is almost here. There's nothing we can do to help." As the agent spoke, a small, slender branch flew off the tree and struck Red Beard in the back.

"There's something I can do. But keep your eyes open. Make sure they don't have an AMR to shoot at us!"

TJ pushed the control stick, and the helicopter dipped down. The rotors tipped and the wind whipped the trees. Branches, sticks and leaves swirled and snapped into the air, pelting the bikers. They scrambled for their motorcycles. But not Red Beard. He reached behind his back just as he'd done in the parking lot when TJ thought he might be reaching for a weapon. Sure enough, when his hand came from behind his back, a black pistol was nestled in his palm.

He took aim. TJ pushed the control stick down and headed straight for him. Red Beard didn't ease up or move away. Agent Belter leaned back and pushed his feet into the front of the helicopter like he was stepping on brakes that weren't there. He yelled something. TJ ignored him as the helo dipped lower. It was a game of chicken as TJ pointed the nose of the helo down and Red Beard aimed up. Her family was in danger. She wasn't going to back down.

At last, a branch full of green leaves broke loose and slapped Red Beard in the face. He flinched and lost aim. As TJ flew over the man, wind and dirt battered him. Shielding his eyes, he ducked and tumbled to the ground. That gave TJ just enough time to ascend. She went high and wide.

As she turned, she saw Trace's truck passing the

farm at a speed too high for someone towing a vehicle. Several bikes pulled out onto the road to follow him. TJ ignored Red Beard and the bikers still parked in the trees. Now she had to protect Trace. She flew over the highway, following him. She went beyond him, then looped around, facing Trace's truck coming straight on.

She swooped low and fast over him. The wind hit the trailer and it weaved dangerously back and forth. But Trace maintained control. The bikers following him didn't. Two men ducked their heads as gravel and dirt from the road's shoulder kicked up and pelted them in the face. One man went shooting off the highway. Another slid and skidded along the asphalt for more than twenty yards. The last biker following Trace swerved and almost crashed, trying to avoid his partner rolling on the road.

Belter shouted their victory straight into the headphones. TJ winced at the loud noise but smiled too. But that was the only concession to success she made. She turned a slow circle back. One of the bikers picked up his motorcycle and headed back to the grove instead of following Trace. The remaining biker helped the injured man. She hovered above them at a safe distance.

A black pickup truck zoomed up the highway. Obviously, it had been hiding close by.

TJ hovered and watched as they loaded the injured man into the back of the vehicle and rolled the bikes up beside him. Then the truck turned and headed back the way it had come.

TJ followed them. "Get the license plate of that truck."

"Watch out! Your friend with the red beard is back." He rumbled down the road toward them, climbed off his bike and pulled out his gun.

"He's taking aim again. What did you do to him to make him so determined to get you?"

"Long story," TJ said as she backed off, out of range. "He can waste all the bullets he wants. I'll just stay up here until they've gathered all their men. Then I'll follow them to their hideout."

They hovered high above the scene below. Disgusted, Red Beard finally stopped firing and, it appeared, got on a cell phone. Soon, another black truck shot up the highway and parked beside Red Beard. A man climbed out of the back seat. TJ recognized the AMR rifle in his hands.

"I have to get higher!" She ascended as fast as she could.

Belter watched over his back and shouted, "Incoming!"

They both held their breath. Nothing happened as the helicopter pulled farther and farther away.

"I'll just stay high so we can follow them."

"Do you know the range of an AMR?" Belter's voice shook.

"No."

"Neither do I. Gomez and the rest of the team are on their way. I suggest we head over to the ranch and let our ground forces handle it from here."

"Sorry, Belter, I can't take that chance. They threatened my family. I'm going to find out where they're based...but I'll stay at a safe distance."

TJ turned the helicopter in the direction of the departing trucks.

FIVE

Trace pulled his truck and trailer beneath the large portico of his family home where his mother waited for them. Eva climbed out of the truck and went straight into his mother's arms. They spoke in low, friendly terms. The scene reminded Trace that they had once been close, before the death of Tara Jean's father had driven them apart.

Neither Chad nor his father came to greet them. Trace was thankful his dad didn't come out, but he wondered about Chad. Was he aware of the preparations for Tara Jean and her family? Had his mother informed his brother? He had to know for sure.

"Mom, where's Chad?"

"He left before ten to go into town. We have a feed shipment that's gone missing."

"Before ten? Did you mention we were bringing Tara Jean and her family to the ranch?"

She shook her head. "No, I didn't discuss it with him."

Trace tried to hide his relief.

"What's going on? Why are you so concerned about Chad?"

Trace dragged his cell phone out of his pocket. "Denby's men knew what we were doing. I want to know how."

His mother nodded slowly as she processed his words. "Chad and Bill were friends for a long time."

He squeezed her arm. "I asked him, Mom, and he denied having anything to do with him. I'm pretty sure he's not involved. I just need to be absolutely certain. I have to protect Tara Jean and her family."

She frowned in concentration. "Have you discussed this with your father?"

"No, I didn't want…" His phone rang. Gomez was on the other line. "Look, if you talk to Dad, don't say anything about Denby, okay?"

She agreed, and Trace stepped away to speak with Gomez.

When he answered, he didn't hesitate. "What's going on? I'm at the ranch and there's no sign of Tara Jean. Where is she?"

"The gang loaded their bikes into the back of a truck and drove it onto a semi. She's following that semi at a distance to see where it stops."

"How far is she going?"

"She has enough fuel to reach the border, but I want her to get back. I have another helicopter en route to take over so she can return. I can't risk losing sight of that semi before the other helicopter intercepts Tara Jean."

Trace shook his head. "How did they know? How could they have possibly known our plans?"

Gomez was silent for a long while. "I don't want to jump to any conclusions. We have a large contingency here at headquarters. Anyone watching our activity could have put two and two together. Also, your family was preparing for your arrival. A worker at the ranch could have alerted the gang. It doesn't mean Chad betrayed us."

Trace heaved a sigh of relief. It was good to know Gomez had the same thoughts. It took the pressure off Trace.

"With you present at the ranch, you'll be able to find the truth and the informant."

Despite all the reassurances that Chad didn't know, his absence from the ranch during the move seemed a bit too coincidental. Why would Chad go all the way into town just for a feed shipment? It made little sense. He was going to get to the bottom of his brother's actions. He was just glad Gomez was giving him time to find the truth.

"What I don't understand is why," Gomez continued. "Why is Denby taking risks like this? Why would he have his men attack you in the open during daylight? It makes no sense. I know we suspected his men wanted revenge for the death of their member. But would Denby risk the whole operation for it? Could he have cause to resent TJ for another reason? Maybe something from the past."

"What could he have against her? She was his victim, not the other way around. We all were."

A cold sensation washed over Trace. "Missy! If

Denby is out for vengeance, do you think he went after her, too?"

"I don't know, but all of my men are here at the Baskinses' airfield." Gomez's voice sounded strained. "I'll contact the local police to see if they can check on her."

Trace thought of Missy's little boy jumping playfully from the porch, and panic shot through him. "You do that. I'm not waiting."

He shoved the phone into his pocket and looked around. His truck was still hooked up to his trailer. He needed a vehicle. He spun and hurried around the portico to the garage. Behind him, he heard his father call his name.

His dad wheeled around to the garage. "Trace, I need a word."

"I don't have time now, Dad. I need a fast car. Where's Chad's sports car?"

"He drove it into town."

Trace's gaze shot around the garage and landed on Chad's bright orange Kawasaki motorcycle. "What about that? Does it work?"

"Sure, Chad still uses it around the ranch."

"Where are the keys?"

"Should be in the ignition, but Trace…"

"I told you, Dad. I don't have time now."

He slid a leg over the bike, flipped the switch and kicked the starter. The motorcycle purred like a deadly cat. Smiling, Trace pulled the goggles off the handlebars, kicked it into gear and shot out of the garage. Unlike the road leading to Tara Jean's place, the Leyton ranch road was paved.

He hit the asphalt and kicked the speed into high gear. He and Chad had spent hours on the ranch's back roads, jumping canyons and climbing hills. When Trace left home, he sold his bike. He hadn't ridden in years. But it was like getting back on a horse. It felt natural. He leaned on the handlebars, coaxing the machine to go faster.

The highway was empty, and he bent low on the turn, barely decelerating, and was back on the gas as soon as he straightened out. Twenty more minutes into town. All he could do as he leaned into the wind was pray that he had enough time to reach Missy and her son.

He wove around cars on the highway, ran a stop sign on the edge of town and shot through an intersection in front of a stopped car. As he turned the corner onto Missy's street, he muttered out loud.

A panel van was parked in front of her house. A man in a leather vest headed up the walkway toward her door.

Trace twisted the handle of the motorcycle and sped up, pouring on the speed. The man was about to step up onto the porch when he heard the revving of the bike. He turned as Trace lifted the front of the motorcycle onto the sidewalk and crossed Missy's green grass.

Startled, the man stepped back and fumbled for something beneath the vest—then pulled out a gun. Trace dropped to the side of the bike opposite the man but never let up on the speed. The man didn't have time to pull the trigger. He dove backward to avoid the motorcycle hurtling toward him.

Trace let off the gas and hit the brake. He placed one foot on the ground as the bike's back tire dug into Missy's grass, forming a deep circle as it spewed mud and grass out behind him.

The man had dropped his gun, and now he scrambled along the ground to reach it. Trace hit the gas again. The bike wobbled, but he held it firm, silently thanking the Lord for his muddy hours on the ranch's back roads. With one foot splayed out, he got his balance and aimed the bike at the man scrambling across the ground. Seeing Trace coming, he fell to all fours and crawled away from the gun. Eventually, he found his feet and ran toward the van.

Trace looked back to see Missy standing in the door just as another man ran from the gate of the backyard with a gun in his hand.

"Get inside, Missy, and call the police!"

Seeing Missy, the man changed direction and ran toward the porch. Trace gunned the accelerator of the motorcycle and headed straight for him. The man stopped, aimed his gun at his adversary and fired. Trace ducked to the opposite side of the bike again, praying the bullet would miss him.

It hit the vehicle's taillight and shattered it. At the last minute, Trace let go of the accelerator and let momentum carry the bike forward. The man lunged out of the way, diving in the opposite direction of the oncoming vehicle. He rolled away. Trace lunged off, and the bike barreled into Missy's rosebushes and stopped.

Trace hit his shoulder hard and rolled. Thankfully, the grass was damp and soft. His landing was not as bad as it could have been. Still, the breath was knocked out of him, and he doubled over. He heard movement and looked up to see the man rushing toward him.

Suddenly, gunfire exploded in the air. The man winced as a bullet hit his arm.

They both looked up. Missy stood on the porch with a .44 Magnum in her hand.

"Get off my lawn!"

The man in the van honked. The biker grasped his arm, spun and ran back to the sidewalk, zigzagging as he went. Missy fired again, but the bullet hit the ground, plowing up more grass. The side of the van was open, and the man rolled inside on his good shoulder. His partner gunned the vehicle and spun it around. The van peeled away.

Missy lowered the gun with shaking hands. "I'm not very good with a moving target."

Gasping for breath, Trace climbed to his feet and bent over, hands on his knees. "That was good enough for me."

He grinned. She gave him a hesitant smile.

"Now get back inside and call the police like I told you."

"They're on their way."

He heard sirens in the distance and nodded. Trace watched the van turn the corner of the neighborhood park. They were getting away again. If he cut across the park, he might still catch them. Hurrying over to the bike, he pulled it out of the bushes and kicked the starter into action.

The engine turned over and Trace patted the tank. "There's a reason Chad's hung on to you all these years."

He backed up far enough to turn around. "Don't open your door for anyone except me or the police, got it?"

Missy nodded and stepped inside. Trace kicked the bike into gear and shot across Missy's already torn-up lawn. He bounced off the sidewalk and crossed the street. The neighbors, hearing the gunfire, had the good sense to stay in their homes. No cars were on the road and no people were in the park. He jumped onto the sidewalk surrounding the park and zoomed across the empty grass. A swing on the playground still whipped back and forth from a child's hasty retreat.

His hometown, quiet little Leytonville, was being turned into a war zone. Trace gritted his teeth and bent over the handlebars. Denby had to be stopped before he turned everyone in town into victims.

Trace jumped the motorcycle off the sidewalk onto the road on the opposite side of the park. He could see the van about two blocks ahead. It made a sharp right, heading out of town. Good. Maybe no more citizens would be endangered.

At that moment, a car entering the intersection screeched to a halt as the van sped through without stopping. The driver sat in the middle of the intersection in shock. Trace had to slow and go around the female driver. She was rapidly dialing numbers on her cell phone. When she looked up and saw Trace, she waved. He knew Etta Corman well. She was his first-grade schoolteacher. Her startled expression made him even more determined to catch Denby and his gang.

He concentrated on the van. They were headed to the business district. Trace's jaw tightened. This time of day there would be lots of traffic in the area, lots of potential for accidents or escape. He needed help. Hopefully Missy would send the local police after him. In the meantime, he had to make sure he didn't lose that van.

He turned the corner and slowed down. The street ahead of him was empty. The van was nowhere in sight. It hadn't been more than a block and a half ahead of him. No way could it have gotten that far away. He scoured the street. On the next block up, a semi was parked in front of a local business. Two more semis were parked on the opposite side, but the van was gone. Trace slowed and eased past the semi to look down the intersecting road. He saw trucks and cars, even a trash truck, but no van. He hurried to the next intersection and slowed again.

The van had completely disappeared.

Pulling to a stop, he looked back the way he had come. A driver climbed into the cab of one semi and started the engine, but that was the only activity on the street. He turned around and went back, scouring both side streets, looking for somewhere the van might have pulled into, but all the business doors were open, and the van was nowhere in sight. All he found were workers and their customers, watching his unusual actions.

He pulled back onto the main street and stopped in the middle. Frustrated, he straddled the bike and let his head hang for a moment. The only moving vehicle on the street had been the departing semi, and it went in the opposite direction the van was going.

Trace had lost them again. He didn't know how they'd disappeared or where they might have gone. What was more, he couldn't figure out how they knew exactly when to stage their simultaneous attack on him, Tara Jean and Missy. How did they know their plan?

At that moment, a car turned onto the street. His brother's gray Porsche pulled up beside him, and Chad rolled down the window.

"Trace! What are you doing zooming around town like a crazy man on *my* bike?"

As TJ and Belter approached the Arizona border, another helicopter took over the pursuit and ordered TJ to fly back to the Del Rio headquarters where Gomez was waiting.

As they climbed out of the cockpit, Belter shook his head. "My legs are shaky, but you look like you could take on a grizzly. You must be made of stone."

TJ made a rueful sound. "Hardly. I just learned a long time ago how to shut down my emotions, especially when there's danger. You can thank Bill Denby for that learned trait."

Gomez greeted her and sent Belter off to file his report, then led the way into the building. "Our people have followed Denby's caravan to a truck stop on the New Mexico border that's packed with vehicles. We think they're going to wait for night to make a switch. We're preparing a ground crew to get there before that happens."

TJ nodded. "Good. I never saw Denby among the riders or the drivers. I don't think he's with them."

"I suspect that's true. I have some photos for you to look at before you leave. We believe the man with the red beard is Alden Brakewith. I'd like a positive ID before I put out an APB for his arrest."

TJ inhaled a shaky breath. She was beginning to feel the effects of her exploits.

Gomez noted her action. "Listen, Tara Jean."

She gritted her teeth at the agent's use of her given name. She could thank Trace for that, and right now, she couldn't afford to be Tara Jean. She needed to be TJ, a pilot—one without shaky legs and trembling fingers.

"Please don't misunderstand me. We greatly appreciate all your help. But I don't want you to take another risk like that. You don't have to go out on a limb. We'll get him."

"I appreciate your concern. But I didn't do it for your case. I did it to get Denby. His men threatened my family, the people I love. I'll do whatever it takes to stop him."

Gomez dipped his head. "Fair enough. I probably would have done the same. Just do me a favor and don't go too far out on that limb. Let us do the heavy lifting and take care of your family. Deal?"

TJ gave him a rueful smile. "I'm not sure I can make that deal. Truthfully, I don't think Denby will let that happen. For some reason, he seems determined to get me."

"That's exactly what we've been thinking. Come on in and let's talk."

He led the way to the conference room where Trace was waiting. He looked worse for the wear. His jeans were grass stained, and he held his shoulder like it was sore.

She stomped on her concerned emotions. No way would she show them right now. She had a bone to pick with Trace.

"What happened to you?" She kept her tone flat.

He sat up in his seat and gave a rueful shake of his head. "Another run-in with Denby's men. They were after Missy, too." She didn't have time to process that info because Trace went on. "I'm supposed to be protecting you. Instead, you're protecting me. We've been discussing how they knew our plans."

In TJ's mind, that was the million-dollar question. She already suspected Chad, and it made perfect sense. He was at the ranch and must have sent word to Denby that they were coming. Her gaze shot to Trace. He gave her a frustrated shake of his head and looked away.

So he was still in denial. That simple gesture made her angry and frustrated. She glared at Trace, daring him to deny what she felt in her bones.

Gomez held up a hand. "Let's not jump to any conclusions, Tara Jean. We already knew they had men watching your place. In addition, anybody here at headquarters could have seen the activity and drawn a logical conclusion that we were moving you. Everyone on the ranch was preparing for your arrival and could have given Denby a heads-up as well. Chad was in town when all this went down. We can't verify that he knew anything about what we were doing. At this stage, we need to find answers, not make guesses."

"Chad and Denby were friends. How much more proof do you need?" Her tone was harsh.

"More than your gut feeling that Chad is guilty." Her tone ignited a hard response from Trace.

They met each other's gaze, and sparks of anger flashed between them.

"Fine. If you want answers, then I'll get them."

"That's my job. Maybe you should back off from these crazy heroics and let us take care of it."

He'd risen to his feet. She stepped closer and stared up into his face.

Those angry sparks now rippled up and down her arms. "If I was sure you would do your job, I'd relax. I'm just afraid you've fallen back into old habits of letting your family members slide by. But let me make one thing clear. Someone jumped you, and my people were in the car. This is the second and last time I'm going to let that happen. I'm just as determined to protect my family as you are yours."

Gomez put a hand between them. "Simmer down, you two. This isn't about whatever happened in the past. This is about Denby and his criminal activities."

His words were like cold water poured over the fiery sparks inside TJ. She blinked and stepped back, suddenly aware of something. Most of those sparks didn't come from anger and fear. They happened because

Trace was so close she could touch him. She wanted to hit him for all the hurt he caused her. At the same time, she wanted to wrap her arms around his waist and hold him. It was a crazy mixture of jumbled emotions that put her over the edge.

That startling awareness caused her to slump and step back even farther. She wasn't thinking clearly. She needed to slow down and sort through her feelings... as far away from Trace as she could get.

Spinning, she walked around the table and sat down on the other side. Trace dropped back into his chair, and both were silent as Gomez moved to the head of the table and laid down the folder in his hand. He linked his fingers together and paused a long moment before taking a deep breath.

"I don't know what went on between you two, but you need to put it aside. Too many lives are at stake."

TJ hung her head. He was so very right. Her feelings surrounding Trace were confused and contradictory. They were getting in the way. She had to put them aside. But that was easier said than done because those feelings went much deeper than she'd been willing to admit.

Gomez went on. "We need to focus on now. I've put in a request for protective custody. If I was sure Chad was an informant, I would do it right now. I've started the process so they will have a secure location in case we need it. But I'm not convinced Chad is our man."

Trace nodded. "I've got my friends, off-duty border-patrol agents, coming to the ranch to help out. I've spoken with my dad. He's put all the hired hands on alert. We've even started patrols around the property."

Gomez nodded. "That's good. But if there's even one more incident, we're going to get Missy—and you—off the property, TJ."

She shook her head. "If I'm gone, how can I help?"

"Like Trace and I have said, it's our job to do the heavy lifting. You need to step back and let us do it."

TJ fumed, still not sure Trace was doing all he could. But she kept silent.

Gomez took a deep breath. "Let's review the facts. We think Denby has a second agenda, but we don't have a clue what it is or what path he plans to take. So let's focus on what we do know. He has a large shipment of arms hidden somewhere on this side of the border. He must get it to Los Desaparecidos, because apparently they've stopped all their regular traffic in anticipation. Two of our DEA agents are heading south to retrieve the body of Denby's gang member and to confer with Mexican officials. It seems they have some new intel about Los Desaparecidos that might be useful to us."

"How long will they be gone?" The frown on Trace's face confirmed he was as worried about the loss of men as TJ.

"At least forty-eight hours. Maybe more depending on the intel, but not much longer. I need them back here. I want all the help I can get."

Gomez turned to TJ. "Tomorrow I want you to start your reconnaissance on the county ranches. Start in the north...this time far away from the border. Work your way south. Any sign of trouble, you call it in, got it? No more chasing after the bad guys."

TJ nodded. "I should be able to finish most of the north sector tomorrow. There are few ranches in that area."

"Good. I'm almost certain Denby's moving his cache. The location you spotted the other day had been cleared out. I think he has multiple hiding places, and he keeps moving them. If we can start eliminating those places one by one, we'll narrow down his options and we'll have a better chance of catching him. But we have to move quick. I get the feeling he's getting ready to make a move. His attempt to capture you-all confirms those suspicions."

"But why?" Trace shrugged. "What purpose does it serve to capture any of us, especially his sister? What does Missy have to do with her brother's stolen weapons?"

"Well, the fact that he attempted to take her against her will proves she's not part of his plans...and she would make a good hostage to get him across the border. Any of you would."

TJ frowned, and a cold feeling washed over her like a flood. Hostages. She hadn't even considered that scenario.

"Chad showing up at that location at the same moment I lost the van has me concerned."

TJ stared at Trace. Was he really doubting his brother's innocence? His concern made her anger moments ago seem even more unreasonable.

Gomez shook his head. "You said it surprised him when you told him Missy had been attacked."

"Surprised isn't the word. It terrified him. He shot out of there like a rocket, leaving me standing in the street. I had to wait for the local police to arrive so I could update them to be on the lookout for the van. When I arrived back at Missy's house, the police told me she refused to open the door for Chad. She didn't come out until they arrived. It was a confusing scene. Missy was keeping Chad at arm's length, and he seemed half out of his mind with worry."

"There's definitely something in their past, and I think it involves Denby in some way. It could be behind his second agenda. What happened between them?"

"I don't know," Trace said. "Chad wouldn't talk to me about Missy then and says even less about her now."

TJ shook her head. "Missy was a victim of her brother, too. He tormented all of us. We didn't dare do anything to him."

"That's right," Trace agreed. "He was dangerously wild. He even turned on Chad in the end. He and Denby threw punches at each other. Chad came home with a black eye and the next thing I heard, Denby left town. Chad wouldn't discuss it at the time, and I was just glad Denby was out of our lives."

TJ sighed. "We were all glad. Little did we know he'd come back and be even more trouble." Her supposition about the past being the key was making more and more sense.

Gomez's features were troubled. "Or that he'd come back with more resources. Those trucks and that semi showing up threw me for a loop. Our information on Denby's gang didn't include that many members. He's either purchased or hired help and more vehicles. That means he owes lots of dangerous people money. He's got to sell those weapons soon."

He shook his head. "The local police are monitoring the businesses and homes here in town. My men are watching the Martinez shop and running down info on Denby's gang, tracing known cell phones and contacting relatives for info on the members' whereabouts… basically anything we can find out. The DEA has tabs on Los Desaparecidos, and state troopers are tracking the freeways and highways. We've got this area almost completely locked down. That'll make Denby a desperate man."

TJ didn't like that thought. In her experience, Denby was dangerous enough without being desperate.

Gomez turned to Trace. "My gut tells me Denby will make a move soon—before we can bring in more reinforcements. Right now, the only weak link we have is not knowing how Denby is getting his information. I need you to find proof of who it is."

Trace frowned but spoke with determination. "I'll get it."

And if he doesn't, I will. TJ nodded at her own silent determination.

"I think it's also safe to say your cover of being off-duty is blown, Trace. I'd like you to carry your service revolver from now on. I don't want you confronting Denby's men again without protection."

Then Gomez turned his commanding gaze on TJ.

"And I need both of you to figure out what happened in the past. Maybe if we have an idea about Denby's second agenda, we can figure out his next step and get ahead of him."

TJ took a breath. "A step ahead. That would be nice for a change."

Because so far Denby had been more than a few steps ahead of them, and he was getting closer and closer to his goal with every step.

Dinner was awkward for TJ. Mr. and Mrs. Leyton were the epitome of gracious hosts. In fact, they seemed excited to have their unexpected guests in their home. Her mother and Judy Leyton talked to each other like old friends—because they were. TJ had forgotten that the Leytons and her parents spent time together when they were younger. She could remember many barbecues and parties her family had attended during her childhood. But her father's death had put an end to their close relationship.

Her mother always told her that John Leyton was her father's best friend, and John had taken his death very hard. Just being around her and TJ brought all the pain back. So their visits grew less and less frequent. It had been that way for many of her mother's old friends. That was why selling their home and moving in with her grandfather had been a blessing for them both—a fresh new location for TJ and a helper for her mother.

Judy and her mother shared a passion for social work and children, so they carried the bulk of the conversation. Missy had asked for a tray to be served to Bobby and her in their room. She said Bobby was having a hard time adjusting, so she also asked if Squirt could join them. Chad missed dinner completely. Trace's parents and her mother sat on one end, and she and Trace sat on the other.

Looking up and seeing Trace in such a casual setting, laughing at something his mother said or teasing her mother, made her more uncomfortable than she could bear. It wasn't that his behavior was fake or wrong. It was just the opposite. Perfect. And that made her even angrier.

As soon as dessert was served, she excused herself, saying she needed to check her helicopter. She went out the back door, through the pool area to the stables. The night was still warm, but a slight breeze ruffled the air just enough to make it pleasant. The moon was full, and clouds scudded over the sky in long shapeless forms. She took a deep breath and inhaled, feeling like she was taking her first full breath of the evening.

She lifted the metal gate of the pool yard and closed it behind her. Hurrying down the gully, she climbed up the next hill and passed the stables to the flat spot beside it where her helicopter was parked. She didn't really need to check the helo, but out of habit, she went through the motions. She dropped open the gauge panel and let it bang against the side. The loud metal echoed over the still night.

"Tara Jean, can we talk?"

She jumped back against her helicopter. "Don't sneak up on me like that, Trace!"

He shook his head. "I made enough noise to scare off that coyote up there on the hill."

She spun and looked at the large hill behind the spread. "There was a coyote up there?"

He heaved a sigh. "For someone whose life has been threatened, you're not very aware of your surroundings. You must have a serious problem on your mind, and I'm pretty sure it's me."

She didn't even try to disagree.

He shook his head again. "I thought you had forgiven me."

Licking dry lips, she studied the moon in the distance. "I tried, Trace. I really thought I had but…"

That strange mixture of want and anger swelled up inside her again. He was close, so close she could touch him. A hint of pine from his aftershave drifted toward her.

She purposely stepped back, right up against her helo. "I'm just not sure I know how to forgive. You say and do all the right things. You've been there twice when I needed you. Just about the time I start thinking everything is all right between us, I get a vision of you standing there while Denby and your brother make fun of me. Or I remember you walking by with Chelley on your arm, and she'd make some smart remark."

He nodded. "You weren't short on smart remarks yourself. But I always thought something else happened between you two."

Yeah, you happened. She gritted her teeth and clamped down on the words.

"Look, I can't change the past, and I'm truly sorry

for the things I did…or didn't do. But I thought it might help if I explained a little more. I had a lot going on at the time. My dad and Chad were constantly fighting. Dad was fed up. It seemed as if he'd given up on my brother and was putting all his hopes on me. Chad saw that, and it was driving a wedge between us. I was fighting to keep my brother from hating me."

He leaned against the helo, and even in the moonlight she could see the pain reliving the incident caused him. He was inches away. "When your grandpa invited me to work on his planes, it was a dream come true. You were smart and capable, a better mechanic than me."

TJ laughed. She couldn't help herself. "Still am."

Once again, his gaze made her pulse beat faster. "You were a better friend, too. For the first time in my life, I knew what it was like just to be me, not the star football player or the richest kid in town. Just me."

He shook his head. "But when school started, everything went back to the way it had been. Chad and Denby were constantly in trouble. Dad was always telling me I was the only one he could count on. I didn't know how to stop the merry-go-round."

"But you did. You jumped off."

"Yeah, and I lost my dad in the process."

She looked away. "I know something about losing your father."

"I know you do. The whole time I was preparing to leave college, I kept building up my confidence by reminding myself how strong and confident you were. You were my hero, Tara Jean."

Reaching across the space, he lifted her chin. "You still are…"

His gaze focused on her lips and he leaned in. He was going to kiss her. Really kiss her.

Once again, her mixed-up emotions began to battle each other. Want, resentment. Want, resentment. Those pesky sparks came to life again and rippled up and down her arms.

Confused and troubled, she jerked sideways—away from his touch, away from the helo and away from her electric emotions.

"You were right. That story does help me to understand you better. But we're still a long way from kissing and making up."

Spinning, she practically ran back to the house.

SIX

TJ leaned against the paddock fencing. The air was cool, perfect for a morning ride. Chad had not made an appearance at the house, but apparently he'd left instructions for their wrangler, Handy, to give Bobby and Squirt riding lessons. Handy came to the house bright and early this morning and brought the boys down to the stables.

TJ was making her preflight check when they entered the paddock. The boys were excited and laughing, so she decided to take a few moments to watch them. She walked down and leaned against the railing.

It didn't look like the session was going well, however. Squirt and Handy had exchanged words. TJ could tell by the expression on the youngster's face the issue wasn't resolved. She had gone to school with Handy and knew him well. He had never been one of her favorite people.

She was considering moving closer when Squirt shouted something at Handy and slammed out of the paddock. He stormed toward TJ, his features set in anger.

"What's going on, Squirt?"

He shook his head. "I don't like that guy. He's mean."

"What did he say?"

"He told me if I can't follow instructions, I should go back to the house."

"So you stormed off instead of doing what he said?"

Squirt's lips thinned. "I was doing what he said. He was just being mean. But I'm not going far. I'm not gonna leave Bobby alone with him."

TJ looked back at Handy, holding the reins of the horse on which Bobby was seated. She remembered the wrangler had a caustic tongue. He was the best with horses, but he might not have been a good choice to teach the youngsters.

"If he's being unkind, we should stop the lessons. Bobby's too young to take that kind of criticism."

"He's not being mean to Bobby. Just me. But I'm still not going far. I'm gonna keep an eye on him. I don't trust him."

Squirt was so like her, unwilling to trust. Still, TJ studied the wrangler. When they were younger, he'd joined in on many of Denby and Chad's practical jokes. She could remember the sound of his cruel laughter as clear as if it had happened yesterday.

"I think you're right. You shouldn't leave Bobby alone. You should go back."

"Mr. Handy told me to go. He says the lessons are

just for Bobby. Not me. Mr. Chad didn't say I should be included."

A deep voice interrupted them. "You go right back there, Squirt, and tell him the lessons are for both of you."

Squirt and TJ spun. Chad had come up to the corner of the paddock a few feet away.

The youngster cocked an eyebrow at the ranch manager. "But he said…"

"He was wrong. And if he gives you any more trouble, you come straight to me."

Squirt looked at TJ. She nodded. Grinning, he took off at a run, grabbing the corner of the fence as he spun around it. He pushed his way into the corral and spoke to Handy. The man looked in their direction, then nodded. He lifted Bobby down and helped Squirt climb into the saddle.

"That kid reminds me of you."

TJ caught her breath and glared at Chad. "Why? Because someone is picking on him?"

He dropped his head and gave it a shake. "No, because he's brave and doesn't back down. He'll never let anyone push him around."

His words caught TJ off guard. Still, she said, "Good. It'll keep him safe from people like you."

"You're never going to forgive me for those years, are you?"

There it was again. That word—*forgiveness*. Was everyone conspiring against her, or was the Lord trying to tell her something?

Dear Reader,

I am writing to announce the launch of a huge **FREE BOOKS GIVEAWAY**... and to let you know that YOU are entitled to choose up to FOUR fantastic books that WE pay for.

Try **Love Inspired® Romance Larger-Print** books and fall in love with inspirational romances that take you on an uplifting journey of faith, forgiveness and hope.

Try **Love Inspired® Suspense Larger-Print** books where courage and optimism unite in stories of faith and love in the face of danger.

Or TRY BOTH!

In return, we ask just one favor: Would you please participate in our brief Reader Survey? We'd love to hear from you.

This FREE BOOKS GIVEAWAY means that your introductory shipment is completely free, <u>even the shipping</u>! If you decide to continue, you can look forward to curated monthly shipments of brand-new books from your selected series, always at a discount off the cover price! <u>Plus you can cancel any time</u>. Who could pass up a deal like that?

Sincerely

Pam Powers

Pam Powers
For Harlequin Reader Service

Complete the survey below and return it today to receive up to 4 FREE BOOKS and FREE GIFTS guaranteed!

FREE BOOKS GIVEAWAY
Reader Survey

1

Do you prefer books which reflect Christian values?

◯ YES ◯ NO

2

Do you share your favorite books with friends?

◯ YES ◯ NO

3

Do you often choose to read instead of watching TV?

◯ YES ◯ NO

YES! Please send me my Free Rewards, consisting of **2 Free Books** from each series I select and **Free Mystery Gifts**. I understand that I am under no obligation to buy anything, no purchase necessary see terms and conditions for details.

❑ **Love Inspired® Romance Larger-Print** (122/322 IDL GRSJ)
❑ **Love Inspired® Suspense Larger-Print** (107/307 IDL GRSJ)
❑ **Try Both** (122/322 & 107/307 IDL GRSU)

FIRST NAME   LAST NAME

ADDRESS

APT.#   CITY

STATE/PROV.   ZIP/POSTAL CODE

EMAIL ❑ Please check this box if you would like to receive newsletters and promotional emails from Harlequin Enterprises ULC and its affiliates. You can unsubscribe anytime.

◆ HARLEQUIN® Reader Service — Terms and Conditions:

▲ If offer card is missing write to: Harlequin Reader Service, P.O. Box 1341, Buffalo, NY 14240-8531 or visit www.ReaderService.com ▼

BUSINESS REPLY MAIL
FIRST-CLASS MAIL   PERMIT NO. 717   BUFFALO, NY

POSTAGE WILL BE PAID BY ADDRESSEE

HARLEQUIN READER SERVICE
PO BOX 1341
BUFFALO NY 14240-8571

NO POSTAGE
NECESSARY
IF MAILED
IN THE
UNITED STATES

"Maybe I could forgive you if I knew you were sincere."

His gaze drifted to Bobby. The wistful, yearning look on his features was painful to see.

"I've paid for my mistakes over and over again."

His tone reflected deep regret. But she still needed answers. "Denby is always one step ahead of us, Chad. Someone is feeding him information. Convince me it isn't you."

He stared at her in shock. "You think I…"

He gripped the railing with both hands. "My family is in danger, too. Do you honestly think I'd endanger my mother and father?"

No, she didn't. But she wasn't quite ready to say those words out loud.

She squirmed beneath the blaring truth of his words. "I need answers, Chad. We all do."

He punched the railing. "You want answers? Here's one. Take your mother and that boy and get as far away from Bill Denby as you possibly can. You hear me? Get away while you're still alive."

With that, he spun and stalked back to the house.

She stared after him. Chad wasn't a friend to Denby, that was for sure. But if Chad wasn't giving the gang info, who was?

There were at least fifteen ranch hands working here. Most of them had grown up in Leytonville, and some of them even knew Denby. It could be any one of them.

TJ sagged against the railing. She was back to square one and time was running out. She could feel it in the air, almost touch it. Denby was ready to make his move. And they were all going to suffer when he did.

Trace disconnected from his call to Gomez. The agent had not given him good news. Telling Tara Jean was going to be difficult, and he hadn't even had his coffee yet. After what happened last night, he was afraid he'd get another blast of anger. He probably deserved it.

He'd always had special feelings for Tara Jean, strong ones, but he didn't realize how deep they went. Last night…he didn't know how it happened. She was so close, and the moonlight lit her with a silver glow. It was like some elemental force pulled them together, connected them. When—or rather, if—they finally touched, it was going to be just like that. Natural. Right. Elemental. And given Tara Jean's personality, a little electric.

Chances were, he wouldn't be getting that close again for a long time, if ever. She hadn't been very happy with him.

He sighed. She hadn't come to breakfast. He was pretty sure she was avoiding him. He needed to make it right because they had to work together. They had a puzzle to solve. There was something they were missing, some piece that might make sense of Denby's actions. If they could just work together, he knew they could figure it out.

They needed to talk, but he was pretty sure the information he had to share with her wouldn't make it a positive encounter. Tara Jean was going to be frustrated and angry. After all her efforts to follow Denby's gang yesterday, he didn't blame her.

He shook his head. No use putting off what had to be done. He went in search and found her working on her helicopter, getting ready for her flight over the north part of the county. She barely glanced up as he walked up. "I think that's close enough."

He looked at the distant hill and counted to five. "Come on, Tara Jean. Last night was a mistake. I'm sorry."

"Seems like you say that a lot to me."

"Yeah, you seem to bring out the worst in me."

That made her smile—a little one, but a smile nonetheless. "You mean perfect Trace Leyton has a bad side?"

"You, better than anyone, know I do."

"Yes, I do. That's why you have to stand over there." There was humor in her tone, and he took it as a good sign. Could it be she wasn't as offended by the kiss as Trace thought? If she wasn't offended, where had last night's intense reaction come from?

"Fine with me if I stand here. I'll just yell what Gomez told me about the FBI raid on the semi you followed to the truck stop."

She stopped and faced him, all teasing and humor gone. "What did they find?"

"Nothing. Absolutely nothing. The black truck, the bikes and all the men, including the driver, were gone. The semi was empty, and Gomez just got the report back. There were no prints, no traces of dirt. Nothing."

She stared at him silently before shaking her head.

"How is that possible? Belter and I saw the truck drive on to the semi."

"It's an old trick, Tara Jean. They had an identical truck sitting under an overpass or hidden from view. When the truck came out from underneath the cover, it was a new truck, cleaned of all prints and evidence."

She sagged. "A second semi." She shook her head. "There was a big overpass as the highway met the interstate. That's the only place they could have switched."

"Yes, and then the semi with the bikers inside would wait until you flew out of sight before they moved. They could have driven to any location in the States by now."

She gave a frustrated jerk of her head. "Red Beard was in that truck. He could be far away. Gomez's APB won't do us any good."

"Don't be so sure. He's put a lot of effort into this robbery. I doubt he's going to let the goods—or the money—get too far away from him."

She heaved a sigh. "I suppose. Belter thinks he has it out for me. I agree. Red Beard's not going to let me go before he gets his pound of flesh."

"You? What did you do to him?"

She gave him a one-sided smile. "Drove him and his bike off the road on that first day when we left the market. I get the feeling he didn't like a female besting him at the wheel."

Trace chuckled. "Or at the controls. You wreaked some pretty good havoc on his travel plans from the air, too."

She nodded slowly. "Yeah, I guess I did." She

slapped the door of the helicopter gauges closed, and he couldn't keep his gaze off her long arms and graceful fingers. It was hard for Trace to remember that she could control a powerful machine, like a plane or a helicopter.

She brushed the dust off her hands. "So that settles it. Red Beard and I have a score to settle."

For Trace, that truth took the humor out of her words. The idea of Red Beard or Denby getting their hands on Tara Jean was too disturbing. They had to be stopped before that could happen…and the only way to do that was for them to work together. He needed to breach the gap between them.

"Tara Jean… Gomez wants us to talk about the past—not ours, but what might be behind Denby's second agenda. Can we talk about that?"

She ducked her head, avoiding eye contact. "Now is not a good time, Trace. I need to get in the air."

He dragged in a slow, frustrated breath. He knew his news would put her in the wrong mood for talking, and now he had more questions than ever. "When is a good time, Tara Jean?"

She threw up her hands. "Trace, I was awake most of the night trying to figure things out. Now I'm tired and I need to fly while I'm fresh. This conversation will just have to wait."

Spinning, she climbed in the cockpit of her helo and slammed the door shut. Before he could even say a word, she had her headphones in place and started flipping switches. Trace released a sigh. The way things were going, they'd never have that conversation and he'd never know what emotions were behind her resistance to his kiss...to him. Did she really dislike being in his arms, or was she just afraid?

He was afraid too. His reaction to her had been more intense, more real than even he had imagined. But she was determined to keep so much distance between them, they might not ever discover the truth.

Frustrated, he stepped back from the helo. The overhead blades whirled, forcing him to walk off the rise. As he came down, Eva walked toward him. Behind him, he heard the blades spinning faster as Tara Jean lifted off.

Eva met him halfway up the hill. "I missed her. I wanted to tell her we have a storm front headed our way."

Trace looked back. "Yeah, I wanted to talk to her too."

Eva studied him before she nodded. "Yep, she's had a bee in her bonnet since she got back yesterday. It's best we let her fly."

Trace chuckled. "I haven't heard that expression in ages, but I guess it suits Tara Jean's mood. She has a bee in her bonnet for sure. But why should we let her fly?"

"Because that's where Tara Jean meets God."

"You're speaking in riddles today, Eva, and I'm fresh out of guesses."

She leaned back. "Trace Leyton, have you seen my garden?"

"Yes, ma'am. It's one of the finest in the county."

"Yes, it is. I like to garden, but that's not why I spend

so many hours there. It's where I meet God. With my hands in the soil and the sun on my back, the Lord and I have our best talks. Wouldn't know how to get on with life without our conversations. Tara Jean has her talks when she's in the clouds. It's best we let her solve her problems up there."

Trace released his breath. "I guess I'm afraid I'm part of the problem."

She studied him again. "Maybe so, but you won't find your answers staring up at her. Where do you do your best talking?"

Surprise filtered through him. He didn't know where he had his best conversations. Maybe that was why the Baskins had made such an impact in his life. They always seemed to know how and where to talk to God. Ever since he was a young man, he'd hungered for that kind of relationship with the Lord. But he never knew how to get it.

He shook his head a bit ruefully. "Well, ma'am. I'm not sure I know where my 'talking place' is."

She nodded. "Don't you think it's about time you figured that out?"

Trace chuckled. Trust Eva to hit the nail on the head. "Yes, ma'am. I do believe it is."

"Good." Leaning forward, she kissed his cheek. "I'm going to go find Squirt and Bobby. They've become the best of friends. It simply delights me to watch those two together. Last time I saw them, they were headed to the barn. Chad asked that young man named Handy to give them a riding lesson."

She shook her head again. "Who names their child Handy?"

Trace laughed. "His real name is Walter, so you can imagine why he prefers the nickname we gave him. We called him Handy because he's handy with horses, always has been, even when we were kids."

That thought triggered something in his mind. Handy had been around the ranch since they were in grade school. Now he wrangled horses for them, but back in the day, Denby counted Handy as a friend, too.

Perhaps it was time Trace checked in on his favorite horse…and not just because he needed to see Handy. He was overdue for a long talk with the Lord.

TJ's flight pattern had taken longer than anticipated. High winds forced her to change her route several times, and she'd been just a little distracted.

She hadn't been ready to talk to Trace this morning for more than one reason. Delving into the past was difficult, but the present was even more pressing. She tried not to show it, but his story about his troubles with his father affected her more than she cared to admit. That made her angry because she didn't need one more reason to care about Trace Leyton. That "push me, pull me" feeling he always created in her didn't need any more shoves. One more just might put her over the edge—though of what, she didn't know.

The truth was, she was afraid. It was that simple. She'd been half in love with Trace all her life…and she'd fought those feelings just as long. If she stopped blaming him, if she really forgot the past and started working with him, would she lose her heart completely?

Gomez's words echoed in her mind. Lives were at stake. Not just hers, but those of her mom, Squirt, Missy and her son as well. She had to put her fears and anger aside long enough to work with Trace. But that "almost kiss" last night had made that more difficult than ever.

She'd been praying all morning and still had no solution. Why couldn't she put the past behind her and move on? It seemed everyone else had—Missy, Trace, maybe even Chad. But she was stuck in the same mode.

It seemed she'd been angry all her life. Angry that she lost her father. Angry that PTSD caused her grandfather to drink. Angry that Trace hadn't cared for her the way she had cared for him.

But now he was showing signs of caring—a grown-up kind of caring—and she couldn't let go of her anger long enough to see where that might lead. She was too afraid it might happen again, and her walls of anger were so thick, no one could break through them anyway.

The Lord had been putting the word *forgiveness* in her path. She knew it meant something. She was supposed to listen. She thought she might even have to forgive, but saying the word and doing it were two separate things. She simply didn't know how.

Today, no matter how hard she tried, no answers came to her. She tried to concentrate on the job at hand, but she'd been so busy thinking, she'd missed several facilities and had to go back and recheck.

Every building she flew over was empty. She found no signs of the gang or any activity, but she finished the northern section completely. She headed home, weary but certain she'd done all she could.

It was late in the afternoon when she finally returned to the ranch. She'd told Trace she hadn't had much sleep, and that was the truth. She landed and stepped out of her helicopter on legs that were wobbly. Her lack of sleep, hours of flying and her mental battles had taken their toll. She was stressed. As she walked back to the house, she heard laughter and the splashing of water.

The metal gate leading to the pool and patio creaked as she opened it. Three smiling faces greeted her. Bobby and Squirt were jumping off the side into the water. The older boy waved vigorously and jumped, and Bobby copied his new friend's actions. TJ smiled at their sweet innocence. It was just what she needed.

Missy motioned her over to sit under the shade of a large red umbrella. TJ crossed, sat down and stretched her legs out on the long lawn chair.

"It's good to see you back safely. Squirt was really worried." Missy smiled.

TJ nodded. "Squirt worries a lot."

Missy shrugged and pushed her dark glasses up on her nose. "So does Bobby. I guess it comes from them both being insecure about their future. Squirt doesn't have a home and Bobby is the only child of a single parent. He worries over me constantly."

The tone of TJ's old school acquaintance gave her

pause. She turned to Missy, but the woman kept her gaze focused on the boys.

"Bobby's father doesn't help support him?"

"Nope. He doesn't even know Bobby exists." Sadness laced Missy's tone.

"I'm sorry, Missy. That must be hard."

She shrugged. "Not as hard on me as it is on Bobby." Her lips sealed tight, and TJ turned to watch the boys. Squirt was trying to coax Bobby into jumping off the side of the pool into water that was a bit deeper.

Missy gave a quick shake of her head. "I want you to know how much I appreciate Squirt. He's been such a help to Bobby. This whole thing would have been a nightmare for him if Squirt hadn't..." She broke off and gave another quick shake of her head. "Please just tell him how wonderful he is."

TJ laughed. "I try to tell him that often. I'll be happy to do it again. I don't think he's had much of that kind of talk in his life."

Missy pushed up her glasses and spoke again, her voice sounding a bit teary. "You and I both know a little about that kind of life, don't we?"

TJ nodded. "Yes, we do." She paused. "I always wondered why you didn't come out to the airfield and become a Misfit with the rest of us."

Missy laughed, but it wasn't a pleasant sound. "The answer is simple. Billy wasn't welcome so he wouldn't let me go either."

TJ looked at her friend. "It couldn't have been easy having him as a brother."

Missy sighed. "Believe it or not, there was a time when he was good to me. But something happened…"

Whatever happened might be the missing piece of the puzzle. If TJ could understand that, maybe she could figure out what was driving Denby. She kept silent, waiting for Missy to keep going. But she stopped talking.

TJ prompted her. "What happened? What caused the rift?"

At that moment, Squirt jumped off the diving board, doubled up his legs and yelled, "Cannonball!"

A huge wave of water swept out of the pool in their direction. Cold water splashed across TJ's and Missy's faces. They both gasped and froze.

Squirt climbed out of the pool and came running. "Sorry…sorry! I'm so sorry!"

"Don't run! You'll slip!" Missy shouted.

The boy froze. Everyone stopped in their tracks, and silence reigned over the pool. Then Bobby, still in the water, began to giggle.

TJ joined him and Missy, too. The only one not laughing was Squirt. He stood shivering in the hot Texas air, a look of horror still plastered on his features.

"Poor kid," Missy murmured under her breath, and rose. She crossed the space and quickly wrapped her arms around him for a hug. "A cooling off is exactly what I needed. Now get back in there and teach Bobby how to do that!"

The grin that appeared on Squirt's face made TJ's heart melt. As Missy walked back, TJ wanted to hug her too. "I think you just made a friend for life."

Missy smiled. "Squirt's easy to be friends with."

TJ shook her head. "I meant me."

Surprised, Missy's head jerked up and she met TJ's smile. Once again, she pushed her glasses back up her nose. "I thought we were already friends."

"I hope so, Missy. I truly hope so."

Missy paused, completely understanding TJ's undertone. She nodded and spoke in a low voice. "If I had a clue what Billy is after, I would have said so from the beginning and spared my son being relocated. I wish I knew more, but I'm as clueless as everyone else."

She slapped her hand across the towels on the end of her chair. "Wow. These are drenched. That was quite a cannonball. These wet towels won't help the boys when they get out. Will you keep an eye on them while I fetch some dry ones?"

Obviously, Missy was done talking. TJ released a disappointed sigh. "Sure. No problem."

"Thanks. I'll get us some drinks while I'm in there."

TJ nodded absently and focused on the boys. She wished it weren't true, but she believed every word Missy said. Her old friend truly didn't have a clue about her brother's intentions. So they were back to square one.

She eased back on her chair and let herself relax completely. The cold water on her warm skin had been shocking in more ways than one. She knew she was overwrought. Being stressed wouldn't help her find the answers she needed.

She released a heavy sigh, determined to wind down. Thankfully, she had the perfect distraction right in front of her. The boys were standing on the side of the pool. Squirt was carefully instructing Bobby how to dive. Squirt cupped his arms over his head and literally fell headfirst into the water.

He came up, shaking the water out of his face. "See. Just like that. It's easy."

Bobby nodded but didn't look confident.

"Come on. Just follow my directions. I'll be right here if you belly flop."

TJ smiled. Apparently, Bobby was up to the challenge. He nodded and shifted his shoulders, and his little chin tightened with determination. His lips thinned and he ducked his blond head in a way that seemed familiar.

As he stood there, gaining courage, TJ realized why he looked familiar. He was the spitting image of a young Chad.

Bobby was Chad's son.

Surprise swept over TJ's body, drenching her in a cold chill.

Of course. It made perfect sense. Chad and Missy were together during the last months of her senior year. Chad and Denby had already graduated. Then right after TJ and Missy graduated, her friend left town. Nobody knew why or heard from her until several years later. If Missy was expecting a child, that explained her abrupt departure. It explained a lot.

Missy returned with fresh towels tucked under her arm and two glasses of sweet tea in her hands. She handed one to TJ.

She met Missy's gaze. "Does Chad know Bobby is his child?"

Missy sagged and released a breath. Dropping the towels, she flopped down on the lawn chair before answering. "No… At least, I never told him. But I knew if I came here to the ranch, someone was bound to notice the resemblance. That's why I tried so hard to stay away. Billy's men left me no choice."

TJ nodded. "I'm glad you came. I think you're safer here than in town."

"I hope so, but Billy's reach seems to be just as strong as it used to be."

TJ decided to take Missy into her confidence. She turned to face her old friend. "Missy, someone is feeding your brother information about our actions. We're trying to figure out who that might be. We think it might be one of his old friends…maybe even Chad."

Missy nodded slowly. "I think I understand what you're looking for. You believe the past might be the answer to why Billy's here. I'll tell you what I do know." She closed her eyes. "I remember my graduation like it was yesterday. Chad and Billy were carousing around town like they owned the place. I didn't tell Chad about Bobby because I knew he'd tell Billy, and I desperately needed to get away from him. I couldn't raise a child around someone as violent and unpredictable as my brother. I begged Chad to take me away, some place where Billy would never find us. When he refused, I knew I had to leave. I had some money put away from working at the Burger Shack, so I packed my bags and left for San Antonio. I would never have come back, but my uncle left his house to me. It wasn't worth much, but it would be a home for Bobby and my brother was gone. I never dreamed he'd come back."

TJ shook her head. "None of us did. Missy, can you think of any reason why your brother would try to take you and Bobby?"

"Honestly, I've racked my brain, TJ. I haven't talked to him since I left that night. But you know as well as I do, Billy doesn't need much of a reason to hate."

"That's for sure. I guess he picked on me because my grandfather wouldn't let him on our airstrip."

Missy nodded. "And he hated Trace because he said he slowed Chad down, made him feel guilty about having fun."

Realization swept over TJ. They'd been looking for a motive for Denby's second agenda. She was pretty sure she'd just found it. Vengeance.

Denby came back to Leytonville for two reasons: to ship his stolen weapons across the border at a place he knew well…and to take his anger out on the people he felt had wronged him. Missy, Trace and TJ were his intended victims. But what about Chad? Was he a willing accomplice to the man who was putting his son in danger? Or was he a victim, too?

TJ intended to answer that question as soon as possible. Maybe even tonight.

Trace had been with Gomez most of the afternoon, debriefing the agents who returned from Mexico. Their intel about Los Desaparecidos was confusing. The Mexican gang was preparing to receive a massive shipment. A specially fitted truck was coming from Mexico to pick it up very soon. The agents didn't know the exact time, but they had one key piece of intel—the exchange was to take place at the Martinez Auto Shop. That made little sense to Trace or Gomez. Why would Los Desaparecidos burn a perfectly good connection on this side of the border by involving the Martinez shop?

The team had a long discussion and consulted with the DEA. Together, they concluded Los Desaparecidos were receiving another shipment, not Denby's weapons. Gomez handed the operation over to the DEA with the agreement that his team would be on hand when they made the bust. In the meantime, Gomez sent Trace home.

He was glad for the reprieve. It had been a day full of conflicting info and tension, and he needed a break.

It was dark, long after dinner, when he arrived at the ranch. Eager to forestall questions from his mother and father, he stopped outside, talking to the FBI agent on guard. Belter told him Chad left early in the afternoon and had not returned. As they talked, Handy drove past the garage to the bunkhouse.

Belter pointed to his passing vehicle. "Chad's been a no-show, but that one's been back and forth several times."

"Handy? I wonder what he's been up to today."

"I don't know. But we've gotten so used to seeing him coming and going we just wave when he passes."

They were standing in the shadows when car lights flashed. Chad drove up and immediately exited his vehicle. He didn't see Trace or Belter beneath the portico. He spun and stalked around the garage toward the back of the property and the stables. Trace signaled to Belter that he was going to follow his brother.

Chad walked to the stables with strong, purposeful strides. Trace followed at a safe distance. The hot day was finally cooling off. The air was comfortable, and the night sky looked like black velvet dotted with a million diamonds. Any other time, Trace would have enjoyed the beauty. But tonight, he was just thankful it was dark enough to hide him.

Chad opened the door, and the light that poured from the barn spilled onto the ground in a square. Trace heard Chad greet someone and hurried his steps so he could peek inside before the door closed. It shut so quickly Trace couldn't catch a glimpse, but he recognized Handy's voice. With the door shut completely, he hurried closer and leaned in, hoping to catch some of their conversation.

"If you are lying to me, Handy..."

"Now, why would I do that, Chad? What good would that do me?" The tone of Handy's voice hinged on some attitude Trace couldn't quite place. He wished he could see Handy's expression. Was he being sarcastic? Sly?

Apparently, Chad felt the same way. "If I find out you've been lying to me, I'll make sure you never work here or anywhere in Val Verde County. You understand me, Handy?"

"Whoohee! Why so serious, Mr. Boss man?"

Trace didn't need to see the man's face to know he was poking Chad. Why was he baiting him? Trace gritted his teeth, frustrated that he hadn't moved more quickly so he could have heard the whole conversation.

His brother's tone was barely contained when he answered. "Never mind about that. Just remember what I said."

Trace and Chad had known Handy since they were kids. He couldn't imagine what might've caused the problems between his brother and the wrangler. More than that, he couldn't explain the sarcastic tone Handy had used. Why would he call Chad Mr. Boss man? Why were they angry with each other?

He was so caught up in the puzzle, he barely heard footsteps coming his way. He caught the sound just in time to duck around the corner. There was no light on this side of the barn. As he groped his way along the side, he bumped into something soft. There was an exclamation. Trace recognized the voice and instantly knew he'd run into Tara Jean. She fell back against the barn, and he grabbed her arms to steady her. Now, with his eyes accustomed to the darkness, he could see her wide-eyed gaze looking up at him. The soft scent of jasmine drifted toward him, and her lips appeared extra pink in the starlight.

The barn door slammed open. Light flashed over the yard, along with the angry words, "Who's out there?"

Any second Chad would come around the corner, so Trace did the only thing he could do. He pulled Tara Jean into his arms and kissed her. Her lips were soft and pliable. She tasted sweet, and she fit in his arms as perfectly as he'd always known she would.

He didn't want to end the kiss even when he heard

Handy's low chuckle, and his brother's disgusted words. "Come on you two, get a room."

The gravel beneath Chad's feet crunched as he spun and stalked away. Despite that, Trace still didn't want to end the kiss.

At last, Handy chuckled again. "Don't mind me at all. I'm enjoying the show."

Only then did Trace release Tara Jean and look at the wrangler. "Find your own entertainment, Handy."

Grasping Tara Jean's hand, he led her down the hill to the paddocks. As the warm darkness enveloped them, he found himself reliving the sensation of her lips and the wonder of what he'd known all along. Tara Jean was meant for his arms.

They reached the paddocks. He leaned against a fence with one arm and glanced back. Handy was still standing in the lit doorway of the stable, watching them. Trace put an arm around Tara Jean and turned her, facing away from the wrangler.

He spoke in low tones. "I'm sorry. It was the only thing I could think to do."

She nodded but didn't speak. Had the kiss shaken her as much as it had him?

It appeared it had, and with that thought, all his thoughts coalesced into one. Tara Jean cared. She'd resisted him—the attraction between them—out of fear. Instead of making him feel better, he grew frustrated. This was a complication they didn't need right now. They had too many other things to deal with... starting with the reason she was out here.

He gritted his teeth. "I thought you were going to let

us do our job. Too much is happening for you to take silly chances, Tara Jean. Explain to me why you still feel the need to spy on my brother."

"I think maybe for the same reason you do."

Trace gave another shake of his head. "I'm trying to prove Chad's not involved with Denby. You're convinced he is."

She touched his hand where it rested on the metal paddock fence. "I'm not so sure anymore, Trace. I think I know why Denby has targeted us, but there's something I need to tell you first."

She looked up at him, her eyes wide.

"What could be more serious than Denby's motives?"

"Trace... Bobby is Chad's son."

Shocked, he stepped back before he remembered Handy standing at the top of the hill, watching them. He stepped back, put his arm around Tara Jean and pulled her closer. Tension and shock rippled through his body. Having her close seemed to help.

"That can't be true. If you're making this up to justify your mistrust of Chad..."

"I was at the pool with Missy and the boys. I saw the resemblance, so I just asked her. She told me he is Chad's son."

Trace shook his head, looking into the distance. "How...how could Chad not tell us? How could he not claim his own son?"

She squeezed his hand. Her soft touch seemed to ease some of the anger building inside him. "Because he doesn't know, Trace. She never told him. That brings me to the reason Denby is after us. Remember how Missy left town right after graduation?"

Numb, Trace could only nod.

"Missy knew she was pregnant. She asked Chad to break it off with her brother, to get his life straight. When he refused, she packed her bags and left."

The events of Chad's destructive past clicked into place for Trace: Missy's abrupt departure. Chad's concern for her and her determination to remain at a distance. Even the fight between Chad and Denby before the criminal left town. They'd probably argued over Missy. Now it all made sense.

The long reach of the past saddened him. The damage from their mistakes never seemed to end. He'd never felt it more than right now, learning that he had a nephew who didn't know his own heritage.

At the top of the hill, Handy yelled, "Y'all are no fun anymore! I'm going back to work."

He stepped back inside the stable and slammed the door. Tara Jean released a sigh and stepped out of the curve of his arm. He felt her absence immediately. Having her nearby had somehow softened the blows.

"I have a nephew," he murmured.

"Yes, and I know the reason Denby hates us all. We were looking for his second agenda. I think it's vengeance. Missy says he hates me because my grandfather banned him from working on the airstrip. He hates you because you always made Chad feel guilty about having fun. The only thing she can't understand is why Denby might have it out for her. She walked away, and they haven't had contact since."

Trace nodded slowly. "Maybe Missy is the reason Chad called it off with Denby. Maybe that caused the fight between them."

"That's what I thought," Tara Jean agreed.

Trace leaned both arms against the paddock fence and let his head droop. Finally, he straightened. "It's time for us to confront Chad. Come on."

He took her arm and headed back toward the house.

Just then, the headlights of several vehicles came over the hill behind them and gunfire erupted from the front where Belter was on guard.

SEVEN

The trucks at the top of the hill stopped. Four men jumped out of the drivers' seats and ran around to the back. Metal banged. Engines revved, and all-terrain vehicles drove down ramps attached to the truck beds.

Trace grabbed her hand. "Come on."

He dragged her down the hill to the house. TJ glanced back and saw the headlights of the ATVs weaving back and forth down the hill. She was so startled she almost stumbled. Trace grabbed her beneath her arms and lifted.

At the same time, he shouted at the bunkhouse. "Wake up! We're under attack!"

When TJ was on her feet again, he pulled her along. Men spilled out the door of the bunkhouse. Some ran back in, then came out with guns. They loaded into their vehicles and scrambled up the hill toward the advancing ATVs.

At last, Trace and TJ reached the back gate. Trace slammed it wide. His dad had the sliding glass door open. "What's going on, Trace?"

"We're being attacked. Where's Chad?"

"I don't know. I heard him shout from somewhere out front. Then I heard shots."

By that time they were inside, and Trace closed the door. Her mom, Judy Leyton, Missy, Bobby and Squirt were all standing in the center of the living room.

Trace took command. "Mom, you and Eva get the boys into the bathroom and lock the door."

His mother nodded and bustled the frightened youngsters away. She glanced back nervously at her husband but must have decided he was in expert hands with Trace.

"Dad, I need you to guard this back door. If any of those men on the ATVs get past the ranch hands, you stop them here."

His dad nodded and wheeled off to get his gun. Sal and Betty ran from their quarters, Sal with a rifle in his hands. "Where do you want me, Trace?"

"By the kitchen door, Sal. They're trying to get to our family. Don't let it happen."

"Not a chance."

Trace started for the door when TJ stopped him. "What about me?"

He shook his head. "I'd prefer you went with your mother, but I know you won't do that."

Mr. Leyton had returned with a pistol and a rifle on his lap. "Dad, can Tara Jean use one of those?"

His dad held both up. "Which one?"

She pointed to the rifle. "I'm more accurate with that."

He handed it to her. "Be careful with my wife's

Creedmoor, young lady. She'll have your hide if you aren't."

TJ took the gun and the box of shells from him and followed Trace to the front door.

"Lock this behind me." She nodded, and he was gone before she could say more. She set the box of shells on a nearby stand and loaded the gun. Then she headed to the sliding glass door.

She looked back at Mr. Leyton. "I'm going to the backyard."

Sliding the door closed behind her, she hurried along the pool. There was a small metal table by one of the lounge chairs. Grabbing it, she placed it up against the back fence and climbed on top.

The ranch hands had formed a line of trucks between the ATVs and the house. Headlights glared up the hill. Single headlights flashed back and forth as the ATVs zigzagged back and forth downward. She could see ranch hands bent over the hoods of their trucks, and shots rang through the air.

The ATVs seemed to bunch up in a circle, as if they were conferring. Then they all turned and went in a straight line, headed for the ranch hands and their trucks, except for one rider. He waited with his headlight off. When the ranch hands were engaged with the oncoming ATVs, the lone rider took off, making his way in a lateral advance toward the house. Faced with the oncoming ATVs, none of the ranch hands seemed to notice the lone rider. But TJ did.

Balancing the heavy rifle on the fence, she found the rider in her sights. She tucked the butt of the gun into her shoulder, secure and tight, then took a deep breath and held it. The rider came forward. TJ waited... ten seconds. Twenty.

Suddenly, the rider turned on his headlight. TJ was momentarily blinded, but only for a second. Readjusting her sight, she aimed for the headlight itself. She held her breath to steady her aim and squeezed the trigger.

The headlight shattered. She saw shadowy movement as the ATV rider cried out and lifted his hands off the handlebars to cover his face. The ATV wiggled from side to side and nearly tipped. But the rider grasped the bar with one hand. The other was still pressed to his face. He jerked the ATV around and shot back up the hill. But not before TJ glimpsed his red beard.

He returned the way he'd come and, as if by some signal, the other riders turned and fled back up the hill and over it. The truck drivers shoved their ramps onto the beds of their vehicles and fled too. The ranch hands jumped in their trucks and followed the attackers until they, too, disappeared over the rise.

Sighing with relief, TJ hurried inside. Mr. Leyton was still seated in the center of the living room. She locked the door behind her and hurried to his side. "Any sign of what's going on out front?"

He shook his head. "All the noise came from back there." He eyed her askance. "I heard you shoot. Hit anything?"

She smiled. "I did some damage to an old acquaintance."

Nodding, he set his jaw in a tight line. "Bill Denby's going to regret coming to my house."

It was true. Gomez had made the right choice in sending them here, despite Missy and TJ's arguments. Denby's small army couldn't get through the protective ring the Leytons and their men had created.

"Do you think it's safe to tell my mom and the others to come out?"

He gave TJ a one-sided smile. "I doubt we could keep those two women in there much longer now that the shooting is over."

TJ hurried to the bathroom and knocked on the door. They piled out of the cramped area and into the living room. Ever-practical Betty came from the kitchen where she'd been standing guard beside her husband, Sal. She asked if she could make coffee and drinks.

Judy clasped her hands in a thankful gesture. "I think that's a perfect idea, Betty. Thank you. We could all use a little something."

Eve plopped down on the couch and pulled Squirt next to her. Missy wrapped an arm around Bobby and sat with him in the overstuffed armchair. They were all silent for a long while.

Finally, Mr. Leyton said, "I'm going out there. I can't stand this waiting."

He wheeled out, and TJ locked the front door after him. Silence covered the room again. TJ went to the large picture window and looked out. The ranch hands were returning from over the hill. They drove around to the front of the house to confer with Trace and Chad.

The attack was well and truly over. She heaved a sigh of relief.

Mr. Leyton was right. Denby and Red Beard were probably very unhappy their effort had failed.

Judy Leyton spoke up. "I'm so proud of Trace, I could bust."

TJ turned. Surprised, Eva leaned back to study her friend. "Is that so? Trace doesn't know that."

It was Judy's turn to be surprised. "What do you mean?"

"He told me he didn't think you were pleased with his decision to become a border-patrol officer."

Judy's shoulders sagged. "When he left, it was a confusing and difficult time. I guess I didn't do a very good job of being a mom. Neither John nor I were there for our boys."

Eva nodded. "It's not too late…for you or for John. Maybe if you two mended some fences and worked together, you could make it up to the boys."

Judy shrugged. "I don't know. So much has happened. I'm not sure they can forgive us."

There it was again. That word—*forgiveness*. It kept cropping up in TJ's world.

Her mother's answering tone was low. "You're both still breathing, aren't you?"

At Judy's wry look, her mother nodded. "Then it's not too late. Jesus died so our sins could be forgiven. The least we can do is try. Forgiveness isn't an easy process, but it's the only way to true healing."

TJ gripped both her arms and turned around to face

the dark window again, pretending her mother's words weren't burning a hole in her heart.

True healing. What exactly did that mean? Trace had asked her for forgiveness. She gave it to him and meant it at the time. But saying the words hadn't resolved her issues. She didn't know how to forgive... where to even begin.

She'd been angry all her life, about everything— life and its unfairness. She used that anger and resentment to build walls. Now those walls were in the way of actual relationships with Trace, Missy...even Chad. She'd been so busy blaming and suspecting him, and now she thought he might be innocent.

Shame washed over her.

"I wish you hadn't stuck me in the bathroom. I could have helped. I'd have shown those guys." Squirt's statement sat in the air, heavy, like a living thing.

He was so like her. They were both misfits, needing sturdy walls so they couldn't be hurt. Feelings made them weak, and misfits couldn't afford to be weak.

Her mother shook her head and placed a hand on Squirt's. "Your job is to protect my heart. What would I do if I lost you? It would break me in two."

The words brought tears to TJ's eyes. Trust her mother to say the only thing that might reach the youngster, and it was so true. Mom's heart was an open door.

Would Squirt take the invitation?

The youngster bristled and for a moment, TJ thought he would turn away, keep the walls intact and fight on. Then his shoulders slumped. Reaching across the space, he grabbed her mother's other hand. "No, ma'am, please don't break. I didn't mean it. My place is right here beside you."

The boy had more courage than TJ. And he was smarter than her, too. He didn't have any need for false heroics, as Trace called them. He was brave enough to reach beyond the walls.

A single tear slipped loose and crawled down her cheek. She brushed it away, awash in emotions she'd tried all her life to keep at bay.

The men knocked at the front door, and TJ hurried to open it. Mr. Leyton wheeled in, followed by Trace and Agent Belter. Mr. Leyton went straight to his wife and grabbed her hand.

"Honey, brace yourself. Chad is gone. Those men forced him into his car and took off. We don't know where they've taken him."

The first fingers of dawn were streaking across the horizon when Trace rose from his bed. He and several of the hands had been out all night searching the roads and checking ranches along the highway for signs of Chad's car. They'd just returned a few hours ago to rest. But he was already awake when he heard sounds coming from the kitchen.

Thank You, Jesus, for Betty! He could use a good cup of coffee before heading out again, and maybe even a bite to eat.

He dressed quickly and hurried to the kitchen. As soon as he walked in, Betty handed him a mug. "Eggs will be ready in ten."

Trace stopped her long enough to plant a kiss on her forehead. "Bless you!"

She patted him on the chest. "Just bring my boy home, you hear?"

Trace nodded. "Yes, ma'am. I intend to."

He was about to take a sip when Tara Jean walked into the kitchen. "Are you ready?"

He paused, coffee mug midair. "For what?"

"We're taking my helo up to search."

"Tara Jean, you don't—"

"Yes, I do." Her statement brooked no argument. He knew that tone and the set of that lovely jaw. She wouldn't back down.

"I need some breakfast first."

She nodded. "I'll be doing my preflight check. Come up when you're ready."

Spinning, she left, and Trace turned to meet Betty's gaze. "Nobody better get in that girl's way today. She's on a mission."

Trace sipped his coffee. *Yes, one born of guilt.*

He knew because the same thing was driving him. Fear and guilt. They had to find Chad safe and sound. They had to.

He wolfed down a breakfast burrito. Betty handed him another wrapped in aluminum foil and a bottle of water. "Make her eat this. Her body won't run on anger alone. She needs some food."

Trace took the items, kissed her forehead again and headed out the back.

The morning air was cool. The sun hadn't fully risen yet, and the sky was still gray. There was just enough light to see. Tara Jean was bent over checking the panel gauges when he walked up to her. She straightened, and he handed her the burrito.

"I'm under strict orders to make you eat this."

She made a face but unwrapped the burrito and took a bite.

"Are we ready?"

She swallowed before patting the helo. "I was afraid stray bullets might have hit her, but she's completely intact. Thankfully, I filled up with fuel before I left headquarters yesterday. We have a full tank."

"Good. Let's get going."

Tara Jean started to wrap the burrito again, but he stopped her with a gesture at the food. "After you finish that."

She made another face but ate the burrito, folded the aluminum foil into a ball and tossed it in the helicopter. She twisted the top off the bottle of water and downed a good portion before tossing it into the back of the helo.

"Let's go."

They climbed in. He fitted his headset in place and watched as Tara Jean flipped switches. The engine revved and the blades began to spin. She did her amazing little dance, balancing the controls, the pedals on the floor with her feet, the cyclic and the collective sticks with her hands. The helo lifted. It was an exhilarating feeling. They rose high in the gray sky.

"I'll follow the highway first. Anytime you see something, let me know and we'll go down for a closer look." Tara Jean's voice echoed over the earphones.

He nodded, and they flew across the ground. Cattle dotted the fields near the highway. The sun peeked over the hills, sending a golden glow over the land. It was spectacularly beautiful. Trace could see why Tara Jean did her praying in the sky. It was the perfect place and the perfect time. He sent up another plea for his brother's protection.

Tara Jean must have been thinking the same thing. "I don't think Denby will kill him."

Trace turned to look at her, but she kept her eyes on the sky ahead of them. "Why do you say that?"

"He wants vengeance, Trace. He wants us to suffer."

"Killing Chad will make me suffer."

She glanced his way. "Me too, Trace. I didn't mean…"

He shook his head. "I know what you meant, Tara Jean. You don't have to explain. I think we both feel guilty. We doubted him, and all the time he was trying to find Denby's hiding place and gathering money to send Missy away."

"What?" She took her gaze off the path ahead long enough to look at him.

He nodded. "I talked to Lyle Hanson last night. His ranch is closest to ours. He said Chad offered to sell him his prize horse. Chad told Kyle he was trying to get Missy and her son out of the area. That day when Denby's men almost took Missy? He'd been at a nearby car dealer. He agreed to trade his car in for cash. The rest of the time he's been searching all of his and Denby's old haunts, trying to find him."

Tara Jean sighed in frustration. "So all of his comings and goings were because he was trying to help us? Why didn't he just tell you that?"

Trace released a slow breath. "I guess he thought I wouldn't believe him."

She was silent for a long time. "You would have believed him if I would have let you. Trace, I'm…"

"Don't, Tara Jean. Don't say it. Not now. We both made a lot of mistakes. We have too much regret between us and right now, all that matters is finding my brother."

He looked the other way, not willing to see the hurt his words might have caused. But it was the truth. They had a lot between them. The mistrust. The angry words. The kiss. Talking about it, even thinking about it, took too much energy away from Chad, and right now his brother deserved all his efforts.

They were silent all the way into Leytonville. They covered every street in town and the outskirts with no sign of Chad's car.

Tara Jean spoke first. "Should we head to the border?"

Trace nodded, still silent. The border and Los Desaparecidos made him think of their dumping ground. If his brother ended up there, he would never forgive himself. He pushed that thought away and concentrated on the land below.

"That's the wash Squirt and I followed the other day. It led to a copse where Denby's gang was hiding. Do you think I should follow it?"

"Might as well. We've looked everywhere else. Besides, if they know we've checked the place already, they might think we won't look again. In fact, we should check all the places you've searched before. They could double back and be there."

She tilted the collective to the right and steered the helo toward the wide wash. They followed it for several miles with nothing—but finally, tire tracks appeared in the middle.

"Look, Trace. Those don't look like old tracks. They look new."

Trace agreed. "How far is that place where they were hiding?"

"I don't know, maybe a mile farther south."

He thought for a minute. "Do you still have the handheld radio set Gomez gave you in case of an emergency?"

She nodded.

"Good. Tell me where it is, then land behind that hill. You're going to let me out. Then when I get into position, I want you to fly down to the wooded area."

"What are you thinking?"

"If you fly over, you'll flush them out. They won't expect me to be on the ground. I have a better chance of getting to Chad if he's there."

She nodded. "Okay. I see the logic in that, but you'll be a sitting duck."

"Not if you're watching out for me."

"What if those tracks are just someone out joyriding?"

"No one in town is out joyriding, Tara Jean. Denby has the whole town frightened and locked down."

She sighed in frustration. "All right. Chances are if they're there, they've already heard us coming."

"All the more reason to put me down. They won't be expecting someone on the ground."

She didn't respond, but he could see her lips tighten in determination. "I'm radioing Gomez our location."

He nodded and slid the headset off. He retrieved the handheld radios from a compartment behind the seat and tuned them to the same setting. He handed one to Tara Jean and tucked the other in his belt. The minute the landing skids of the helicopter touched the ground, he leaped out of the cockpit and signaled for her to take off. Tara Jean dutifully worked the controls, and the helo rose. She hovered over him.

"Can you read me?"

He watched her lift the handheld radio. "Loud and clear."

"Let's hope it stays that way."

"Don't get too far away from me and it will."

Trace didn't bother responding. They both knew he would do whatever it took to save his brother.

He ran up the hill and lay down at the top. The wash was less than a mile away. He could see a thick copse of trees ahead, the one the gang had used before. There was enough ground cover between his hill and the wash. He thought he could make it across the distance without being exposed.

Lifting the radio, he punched the button. "I'm going across. Make your way to the wash slowly."

"I'll weave back and forth, make it look like I'm searching."

He released the button, tucked the radio into his belt and took off. He heard the helo fly over him, but he didn't look up. He concentrated on running from one mesquite bush to another. When he reached the edge of the wash, the lip was too high to see over. He dropped to the ground and pushed on the radio.

"I'm here. Fly over the wash and tell me what you see."

He watched the helo fly over, and soon Tara Jean's excited voice came over the radio. "It's there, Trace! Chad's car is in the middle of the wash. It's just sitting there buried in sand up to the wheels with the doors wide open. I can't see if there's anyone inside."

Something about the car being right out in the open caused his senses to tingle. It felt like a trap. He crawled up the lip of the wash and peeked over, studying the trees across from him. Sure enough, he saw the glint of a metal gun barrel.

It was a trap. That long barrel looked like an AMR. They were waiting for Tara Jean to fly over so they could bring her down.

Lying flat, he took careful aim at a spot just behind the rifle barrel. Taking a deep breath, he steadied himself and fired. The rifle went flying and a man landed on the ground. Branches parted, and another man jumped out from hiding to retrieve the AMR. Trace fired again. The man leaped back behind the bushes, leaving the AMR on the ground.

Trace couldn't see the man anymore. He didn't know how many others might be hiding in the clump of trees. Suddenly, a bullet whistled past him, spraying him with dirt and sand. At least they were firing at him, not Tara Jean.

Another bullet drilled into the ground, closer this time. He rolled to the side and ducked behind a large boulder. Even from the different angle, he could not see the shooter. The man fired again. The bullet hit the rock, and a splinter flew off and struck Trace's cheek. Warm blood dripped down his face. He couldn't risk rising to see the shooter or fire back.

The radio squawked. Ducking down, he pulled it out of his belt.

"Tara Jean, can you see the shooters?"

"Yes, there's only one, and he's lying flat behind a bush. The other man's down and hasn't risen."

"I can't see either of them."

"Hold on. I'm going to expose him."

"Tara Jean…"

She clicked off before he could argue. Suppressing his frustration, he waited. He could see the helo dipping down. She was going to use the blowback from the rotors to expose the shooter.

Trace gripped his gun. The helo dipped even farther below his view from behind the rock. He had to risk exposure to see. Leaning out slightly, he looked across the wash. Wind from the copter was kicking up dirt and branches. Shielding his eyes, the shooter rose and turned to run deeper into the copse. Trace leaped to his feet, aimed and fired. The man went down and didn't rise.

Tara Jean hovered, kicking up sand and branches. Even if the man wasn't hurt badly, she was keeping him pinned down. Trace ran to the edge and jumped down the eight-foot embankment to the sandy wash. Kicking up dirt behind him, he hurried to Chad's car.

It was empty. Except for the blood splashed across the inside of the windshield.

Trace spent most of the afternoon in the Leytonville headquarters with Gomez, debriefing. The two men he'd shot were in the hospital. One was in serious condition; Trace's bullet had pierced his lung, and he was in surgery. The other gang member had a wound in his leg and was in police custody in his room. Gomez had already interviewed him, but the gang member wasn't talking. He refused to say anything about Chad's or Denby's location.

Trace suspected the man wouldn't talk, but he'd hung around anyway, hoping. They'd taken a sample from the blood in Chad's car and sent it to the lab, but it was too soon for a report. Trace was exhausted, physically and mentally. The only thing keeping him going was the thought that there wasn't enough blood in the car to be a fatal wound. Chad was still alive.

At least, Trace had to believe he was.

Gomez had been in a meeting with DEA agents for almost an hour, but he finally returned to his office and sat down behind the desk. "The men sent out for pizza. You should grab some before you head home."

Trace shook his head. "I'm not going to the ranch. My guess is the DEA had you in there because they finally got word that Los Desaparecidos' shipment is on its way."

Gomez nodded. "We got word the truck left Mexico about an hour ago."

"That's what I thought. I'm going with you on the raid. If a shipment is going back to Mexico tonight, Chad might be with it."

Gomez agreed. "I figured that's what you'd say. But you're not going back into the field in the shape you're in. If you want to go, you need some sleep. You can use my office. I'll be conferring with the DEA guys. I'll call you when it's time."

Trace grinned to show his appreciation. It was all he could manage. He grabbed a couple of pieces of pizza, then fell on Gomez's lumpy sofa and crashed.

He woke up once to check the progress. Men were spread out on chairs and on the floor of the small facility, waiting. After the call to mobilize, the vehicle they were monitoring stalled on the side of road just this side of the Mexican border. As time dragged on, the team members found places in the department to bed down. Trace went back to Gomez's couch and fell asleep again.

Hours later, lights flipped on in the rooms. Gomez entered, slipping into his Kevlar vest. "Rise and shine. Our truck is on the move again, headed straight for the Martinez shop."

Trace glanced at his watch: 4:30 a.m. They'd been waiting almost seven hours. He sat up, leaned his elbows on his knees and his head in his hands. Now that he was rested, his mind was clear and something about the raid seemed off. Border-patrol officers had not collected any information on Los Desaparecidos in three years. How was it that Mexican officials suddenly had not only info, but the exact time and location of a drug shipment? The entire operation felt wrong.

He expressed his concerns to Gomez. The agent agreed, but since this was their only lead, he felt compelled to follow it. The DEA would act with or without the FBI, and Gomez wanted to be a part of it—no matter what happened.

"Besides, letting the DEA take over leaves my men free to take care of anything else that might come up."

Inhaling deeply, Trace nodded. Then he grabbed a cup of coffee, splashed some water on his face and followed the agent out of the office. In the main room, he slid his vest into place and checked his service pistol. Sliding a magazine into his weapon, he checked the safety, holstered the gun and headed out.

In the parking lot, Gomez motioned him forward. "I thought you might want to know that our men at the location have not seen hide nor hair of Denby or his men."

Trace nodded. Gomez was confirming his suspicions. Whatever this was, it was not Denby's operation. But he still had one question. "Has there been any sign of Chad?"

Gomez shook his head. "That's the only good news I can offer you. No sign of your brother. As far as we know, he's not in the hands of Los Desaparecidos."

Trace shrugged. "Not yet anyway."

Gomez grasped his shoulder and squeezed. "One way or another, we're going to get some answers this morning."

Trace agreed. He just hoped they were the ones he wanted.

They loaded into the back of the Drug Enforcement Response Team vehicle and drove through the sleepy streets of Leytonville. Two weeks ago, if anyone had told Trace he'd be traveling through the quiet streets of his hometown chasing a madman, he would have laughed. But there was nothing laughable about this situation. His world had turned upside down, and he wondered if anything would ever be right again.

The truck stopped several blocks from the auto shop. The DEA agents piled out and moved down the streets to different locations.

"We hold here until the team has the place locked down." Gomez kept his tone low.

"Hurry up and wait again. The story of my life."

Trace saw Gomez's grin flash, even in the dark. "The story of every law officer's life."

Trace returned the smile. No matter what the outcome of this investigation turned out to be, Trace had enjoyed working with Gomez. He hoped they both came through it alive.

Gomez touched his earpiece. "The location is secure. Let's move closer."

Trace led him down a back street to a corner. They could see the Martinez shop ahead. Both men backed up against the building corner as a garage door opened, revealing a bright light. It flowed out of the shop onto the street. Trace recognized the man lifting the door.

"That's Martinez," he whispered to Gomez.

"As far as we can tell, he's not a member of Los Desaparecidos… At least, he doesn't sport the tattoos or markings. But we've connected every one of his male relations to the gang. Because he's so clean, he's been able to float under the BPS's radar."

"After tonight, he'll be out of business."

Gomez touched his earpiece again. "They're making their move."

A small truck drove down the street. Its headlights flashed over Martinez, and he waved. The driver pulled into the shop. Martinez lowered the door, and dark night reigned over the scene again.

"It's a go." Gomez held his breath as men came from different streets and converged on the shop. Shouts of "DEA! Open up!" echoed over the air. There was a long pause before Martinez, arms raised, opened the glass front door of the building. Gomez and Trace waited, letting the team secure the area. At long last the garage door opened again, this time pushed by a DEA agent. He motioned them forward. Not a shot had been fired.

Gomez drew his weapon and hurried across the street. Trace followed more slowly. He stood outside in the parking lot, looking on as agents moved over the truck and began scouting the facility. Only two men were present, the driver and Martinez. When the man saw Trace, a sly smile spread over his features.

"Well, imagine that. Mr. Leyton is back for a visit. What a surprise."

An agent placed handcuffs on Martinez and spun him around. His knowing smile put Trace on edge. Martinez seemed very unconcerned for a man who was about to be arrested for shipping drugs. Trace was beginning to feel sure they would find nothing. His fears were confirmed after they opened the truck—it was empty.

The DEA agent in charge shouted, "Bring in the dogs! We need to know for sure!"

Trace already knew. There were too few men at the shop. If the truck contained a shipment, there would have been guards everywhere, outside and inside. Frustrated, he stepped out of the building and crossed the street. He heard Gomez tell the dog handlers to check the junk cars in the back. There was a large fenced-in area of derelict vehicles and stacks of tires behind the shop, but Trace already knew they wouldn't find anything. More importantly, there was no sign of Chad. Trace didn't know if that was good or bad.

He leaned against the building and shook his head. Martinez wasn't worried because there were zero drugs to find. Their search warrant and this massive effort would yield nothing. It was a setup. But why? Why create this elaborate venture starting in Mexico and moving all the way across the border to Leytonville? He shook his head again.

Suddenly, he saw movement to the side of the shop. A man jumped the fence and ran down the street.

Trace shouted, "Stop!" Then he cut sideways across the street.

Startled, the man stumbled and fell. Trace got a good look at him. He was young, just a kid. He'd probably been hiding in one of the derelict cars in the back.

The young man climbed to his feet. In his hand was a long knife.

He was just a kid, but a dangerous one. He sliced the knife in the air toward Trace's stomach. He lunged back but didn't have time to draw his weapon because the kid charged forward. Trace danced to the side and swung his arm down on the kid's arm. But his slap didn't have enough force to dislodge the weapon. The kid swiped back and again. Trace narrowly dodged the deadly blade.

He didn't have time to make a move. The kid lunged again. This time Trace moved into the kid's reach, letting the knife pierce his vest. He felt the blow strike his left side near his stomach, and he grunted. It was painful, but not painful enough to stop him from swinging his right fist.

The punch connected with the kid's jaw. His head flew back. His knees buckled, and he fell straight down. The knife clattered to the ground. Gomez and several other agents came running up.

"You all right?"

Trace kicked the knife far away, then looked down to examine his vest. The outer layer was torn but the mesh beneath had held. Thankfully.

"He's just a kid."

"Yeah, we found some clothes and personal items in a car back there. It appears he was living inside it. Probably has nothing to do with the Martinez operation."

Trace nodded as the other agents lifted the groggy young man and carried him to a waiting ambulance. "You know, we're not going to find any drugs."

Gomez nodded. "Yeah, I kind of figured that out

when Martinez greeted you like he had been waiting to see you."

"This was a setup, a decoy to distract us."

Gomez looked beyond the shop to the dark hills behind Leytonville. "Exactly. Wherever Denby is, he's making his move."

Tension filled Trace. "I've got to get back to the ranch."

"Go. Take four more agents with you. I'll follow with the rest of my men as soon as we finish here."

Gomez called the names of four agents, but Trace didn't wait. He took off running toward the FBI vehicles parked several blocks away.

TJ woke to the sounds of cooking in the kitchen. She dressed and hurried out, hoping to see Trace. But only Betty was there, starting her morning breakfast preparations.

"No sign of Trace?"

Betty shook her head. "Are you hungry?"

"No, but I'll take some of that coffee, and one for Agent Belter too." If Trace hadn't returned, then chances were the team had staged the raid. That meant Agent Belter hadn't been relieved yet. He was probably exhausted.

The agent was sitting in a chair in the sun, dark glasses in place as his gaze roamed over the hills.

When TJ came out the door, he rose and eagerly took the mug from her hands. "Thank you. I think I could love you."

TJ giggled. "That's because you don't know me very well."

The agent smiled. "But I do. I flew with you. You have a little too much daredevil in you for my tastes, though."

She nodded. "I know someone who would agree with you." Trace's face flashed through her mind. "Still no word?"

He shrugged. "Not even a squawk on the radio. There's been nothing but silence since early this morning."

She pointed to the oncoming clouds. "Do you think Trace or Gomez would object if I flew today? I need to cover the rest of the southern section now if I'm going to beat that storm."

The agent studied the clouds for a long while before nodding. "I've received no orders to the contrary, and it's been super quiet around here since the attack. Just be careful."

"I will. All I have left is the Leyton property. I probably won't even leave the ranch boundaries."

"Just stay in touch with the flight center at headquarters. That looks like a pretty nasty storm."

She hurried inside to change into jeans and a long-sleeve shirt. If it rained, she might need a little something warmer. She passed through the kitchen and grabbed one of Betty's biscuits, hot out of the oven. She tossed it back and forth in her hands to cool it.

"Don't you think you should sit and have a proper breakfast someday?" Betty called after her.

"Maybe, but not today."

Betty clicked her tongue. "Well, I'm sure your mother's going to have something to say about that."

TJ smiled as she headed out the door. Betty was right. Mom would have something to say. That was why TJ had to get in the air as soon as possible. If she could just cover this last section of the Leyton ranch, she might find Chad or some sign of Denby. It was the only place she hadn't checked.

Her preflight inspection took less time than usual. She climbed in the cockpit, put on her headphones and contacted the flight center with her flight plan.

"Got it, TR-22," the controller answered with her call sign. "Stay in contact so we can update you on the storm's progress."

"Roger that."

TJ flipped off her radio, placed her feet on the rotor pedals and lifted off. It felt good to be doing something, to be active instead of just waiting. Yesterday afternoon, after returning from the shoot-out at the wash, she'd nearly gone out of her mind waiting for Trace to call. Of course, when he did, it was only to speak to his parents and update them about Chad.

The sun hit her full in the face. Turning the helicopter into it, she headed east to the far reaches of the Leyton ranch. She traveled over hills and open stretches. It had been a hot, muggy summer with more than usual rainfall, so the brush was thick. A carpet of green lay over the hillsides. Leyton cattle congregated in groups around water tubs, with one herd stretching over an entire hillside.

Looking at the map taped to the control panel, she realized she'd reached the eastern border of Val Verde County and the Leyton property. It was time to turn south. So far, she hadn't seen a single building or any type of wooded area where a truck or van could hide. She was a little disappointed and wondered once again about Trace's progress.

She passed another herd of cattle. The animals moved toward each other, gathering in a circle, a sure sign of a storm coming. She had to hurry if she was going to cover the entire ranch before she had to head back. She was about to call in for a weather report when she noticed heavy tracks, like the ones left by the gang at the border. She dipped down for a closer look, and sure enough, the tire treads were deep and wide, like those of a good-sized truck.

She dipped down a little farther and followed the tracks as they circled around more hills heading south.

"TJ, this is headquarters, do you read me?"

Punching the call button on her headphones, she opened her mic. "I read you. What's up?"

"That storm in the west has changed direction. It's headed our way. We've received early reports of hailstones. We're expecting a tornado warning. You need to head back."

TJ inhaled. She couldn't go. Not yet. She had to follow the tracks. If they led her to Chad…

"TR-22, did you read me?"

"Copy that. I've just discovered heavy tracks that need to be investigated." She read them her coordinates, then said, "I'm heading south, so I'll follow them for a little while longer, then I'll cut west to the ranch. That's the shortest route."

"Roger that. Move quick. The storm is picking up speed."

TJ signed off. The controller was right. Moments ago, the sky had blue patches. Now thick, dark clouds marched toward her.

She ascended above the hills and headed straight south. The tracks led away for miles. If TJ remembered correctly, there was a butte to the north that traveled the length of the county. They could have come from the east and crossed the whole county without being seen. She grew excited, certain she was going to find something.

Strong winds buffeted her helo. If she didn't turn around soon, she might not beat the storm back. In the distance was a large hill that she couldn't see over. She'd just need one quick look at the other side, then she'd head back.

Rising higher, she aimed for the hill and a good look beyond it. As she got closer, she caught a flash of a metal roof just before clouds covered the last of the light slanting from the east. She flew over the hay barn, and on the opposite side, parked in front, was a black truck. The bed of the truck was loaded with crates, partially covered in canvas. Men moved from the almost empty barn to the truck, still loading.

TJ hovered, hoping she could identify some of the men.

Suddenly, another man stepped out from the shad-

ows of the barn. It was Red Beard. In his arms was another AMR rifle. The weapon bucked and TJ shifted,
the controls rising as quickly as possible. She circled
west toward home, tipping to turn the helo as much as
she dared and praying all the way.

"Mayday! Mayday!" She glanced at her coordinates
and shouted them over the mic. "I've discovered the
cache of weapons at this location on the Leyton ranch.
I'm being fired upon. Making my—"

A bullet hit the top of the helicopter. Metal screeched.
Her radio went dead, and the main motor coughed and
died.

TJ punched the ignition and pumped the controls.
The engine sputtered to life again. She breathed a sigh
of relief.

But it whined in a pitchy scream that grated on TJ's
already thin nerves. She knew that sound. If the engine
stopped, there would be no starting it again.

She scanned the landscape below. Up ahead was
an open area. A long enough stretch where she could
land, if she could make it.

The engine sputtered into silence. The helicopter
dropped. The main rotor began to autorotate, spinning
to keep her elevated as the helicopter glided toward
the open area. The autorotation kept the copter gliding
and moving in the direction she needed. She worked
the controls of the back rotor, praying she could reach
the open stretch.

A gust of the stormy wind hit the helicopter and
shoved it downward. It hit the ground, bounced up,

tipped and crashed to a stop with a jerk as the top rotors plowed into the dirt.

TJ slammed against the seat harness and cried out as her chest and ribs exploded with pain.

EIGHT

Trace and the other agents had stopped at headquarters so Trace could retrieve his truck. Now they were following behind him in an FBI vehicle. As he came over the hill that led down to the ranch house, he studied the black clouds just ahead. The storm was going to be a doozy. Automatically, his gaze jumped to the spot next to the barn where Tara Jean's helicopter should have been. He suppressed an angry word as he saw the spot was empty.

She *would* fly and try to save Chad on her own. Of course she would. A storm was on the way. Denby was making a move, and Tara Jean would be right in the middle of it all. He gunned his truck and sped down the hill. He pulled to a stop beneath the ranch house portico. Agent Belter was nowhere to be found.

Trace ran into the house. His father was sitting by the sliding glass windows.

He turned to Trace. "I'm glad you finally showed up."

"What's happening?"

"Agent Belter just got word that Tara Jean's helicopter went down. He tore out on one of the quads, headed in her direction."

"Which way did he go?"

His dad pointed to a dirt road leading southwest.

Trace ran to the front door. The other agents had just exited their vehicle. He shouted at them, "Monitor the house! I'm going after Belter!"

As Trace ran back to his truck, his dad called out, "Be careful, Trace. We just received word that the weather bureau is issuing a tornado watch."

Trace climbed in his truck. He backed up and left the house, kicking up dust and dirt behind him as he crossed the field, leading to the south pasture.

He zoomed around the paddocks just as lightning lit the sky ahead. Tornados didn't hit their area often, but the hail in this part of the country was always dangerous. He bumped onto the trail and hit the gas. A mile ahead, he could see the dust kicked up by Belter's quad. The wind was picking up and blowing violently. Belter was heading into the storm with as much determination as Trace felt.

Trace floored the accelerator to catch the agent. As he gained on the dusty trail, the wind suddenly stilled. Trace glanced at the black clouds above. The storm was directly above him. No wind was a bad sign.

Without warning, large, lemon-sized hailstones fell. Through the windshield, he could see Belter. The agent jerked to the side of the dirt road as the heavy hail pelted him. He climbed off and bent down next to the quad to shelter his head with his arm. Trace raced ahead and pulled up beside him.

"Get in!"

Belter leaped up, but not before a large hailstone hit his arm. He grunted in pain as he slid into the front seat, rubbing his shoulder. "Thanks for coming after me. It was stupid to take off like that. I knew the storm was coming."

Trace shifted into gear and gunned the accelerator again.

Hail pelted the roof of the truck and bounced on the dirt ahead of them. The noise was so loud Trace almost didn't hear Belter's next words.

"I just heard that Tara Jean's helicopter went down near the southeast section." He massaged his arm. "She said something about weapons before her radio went dead."

His words confirmed everything Trace and Gomez feared. The Martinez raid had been created as a distraction to pull most of the law out of the way so Denby could make his move.

Trace swerved to avoid a tree branch blown across the road by the wind. Agent Belter grasped the dash to keep from sliding across the seat. He groaned and rubbed his sore arm as Trace swerved the truck back on track.

Trace shook his head. "I should have known. There were only two places we hadn't searched. Our own land and…"

Lightning struck the road ahead with a brilliant

flash. Trace winced and looked away. He let off the gas, but just long enough for his vision to return.

"We hadn't searched our own land and Tara Jean's airstrip. Those are the only two places Denby could have been."

Trace tightened his jaw and focused on the road ahead. "Denby's men have been hiding in plain sight, here, close to us and at Tara Jean's place where we've already been. I should have realized…"

The truck crawled up a hill. The hail came down like a jackhammer on the roof, and the back wheels of the truck slid backward. The truck didn't move. All four wheels were slinging mud behind them like a dog in a hole. Soon the whole truck began to slide backward.

Trace gripped the steering wheel tighter. Belter grabbed the handle above the door as the truck continued sliding…all the way to the bottom of the hill, where the back wheels bumped over a rock and bounced to a stop.

Belter released his grip on the dash. "Great. Now what?"

Trace barely spared him a glanced. "We go around."

Shifting the truck into four-wheel drive, he revved the engine. Mud flew behind the truck. Power surged them forward, but only slightly. Then one tire caught, and the truck's back wheel plowed over the rock that had stopped their downhill slide.

Belter let out a whoop. Trace shifted into gear and zoomed around the hill.

Dazed, TJ tried to draw a breath, but her chest hurt so much, she froze. A moment passed before she realized why she was hurting. Her upper rotor tips were buried in the dirt and the cab was tilted. She was facing downward, pushed against her seat belt and harness. She tried to release the belt, but it was jammed. She couldn't get it loose and couldn't breathe. Her lungs burned. Stars exploded in her vision. She needed air.

Bracing her hands against the console, she lifted her body enough to release the pressure. She took several deep breaths until her arms couldn't hold her up anymore, and she fell back against the harness.

Her ribs screamed in pain. They were either broken or badly bruised. She had to release the pressure.

Gathering her strength, she pushed up again. There was just enough room to get one leg against the console, so she braced it there and pushed. Grabbing the belt above her head, she got her other leg against the console and with both legs, pushed her body back as far against the seat as she could. The pressure on her chest eased. She breathed deeply, resting her forehead against her knees.

After a few minutes, she raised her head to take stock. The tail end of the helicopter pointed up in the air. The cockpit was facing the muddy earth. The windshield was shattered, and rain was leaking in. Even over the heavy pounding of the rain and the thunder, she could hear the rumble of motorcycles.

The gang was coming to finish their handiwork.

She looked around the cockpit for something sharp to cut the belt, anything to jam into the latch to force it open or break it, but she couldn't reach anything. To her left, men came over the top of the hill, braving the pelting rain. They were determined to get her, and they had large weapons in their hands. She was a sitting duck.

She carried a holstered .22 Ruger pistol attached to the bottom of her seat for protection. It wouldn't be much help against their stolen Uzis, but it would do some damage…if she could reach it. Pushing her legs against the console, she leaned as far to her left as the belt would permit. Her seat was damaged and loose on that side; it wobbled precariously, tilting her sideways against the belt. Pain shot through her chest again, but she ignored it, pushing her body to the limits of her tolerance. Her fingertips grazed the leather holster. She wriggled and twisted, but she couldn't get a grasp on the holster or the gun.

The men continued to march down the hill toward her. TJ was grasping the belt, trying to get beneath it and reach for the gun, when hail began to fall. She watched in amazement as large hailstones pounded down on the men. One was struck in the head and fell to the ground. His partners helped him to his feet. Turning, they carried him back over the hill to shelter. Another man retrieved his weapon from the ground, then, in frustration, swung and fired at her. The gunfire flashed in the gloomy air.

TJ screamed and leaned away, desperate for cover she couldn't reach. Bullets raked across the top of the windshield, missing her, but cracking it even more. Then the man spun and followed his partners, running to escape the ever-increasing balls of hail.

TJ heaved with relief, trying to hold herself away

from the belt as her body automatically took deep, compulsive breaths. But her relief was short-lived. The large frozen hail pounded the windshield, and another crack split down the middle of the shield. If it gave way, she'd be exposed to the hail. Defenseless, with no way to reach protection, she'd suffer even more injury. If one struck her head, she'd be knocked unconscious and lose her footing. She'd suffocate, dangling there by the belt.

Frantically, she searched the cockpit again, looking for something, any kind of tool she could use to work on the belt. But there was nothing. Helpless, she watched as the frozen stones pounded the windshield and tiny spiraling cracks splintered outward in ever-growing circles. Cold water leaked through and dripped onto her head. As a rivulet of water ran down her face, a whimper escaped her. Hot tears flowed down her cheeks and onto her knees as she bowed her head once again.

"Please, Lord. Don't let it end like this. Let me live. Let me tell Trace how I feel about him. Give me the chance to make it right."

She cried softly for a long while until she realized the heavy pounding of the hail had eased into the soft sound of rainfall. Rivulets of water still ran down her head and into her eyes and face, but the heavy pounding of hail on the windshield had ceased.

Closing her eyes, she lifted her face up and whispered, "Thank you."

Soon she heard motorcycles revving up their engines and moving away. She opened her eyes. The dark line of the storm severed the sky in two. One side was gray, the other black. Her helicopter rested on the gray side of the storm, and she sagged with relief. The main part of the storm had passed, and the gang was making good use of the break in the storm to get away. She was safe…for now.

It hurt too much to hold her head up, so she let it drop to her knees again and rested. It was good to know the gang was going away, but she couldn't help but wonder if they were taking Chad with them. Was he this close and she couldn't help him? Guilt gnawed at her.

Then the noise of an engine rose above the soft sound of the falling rain.

Was the gang coming back to finish their job? Her body tensed. Her gaze scoured the surrounding hills. A white truck came from the opposite direction of the gang. She squinted, trying to see through the rain and broken glass. She finally recognized Trace at the wheel and sobbed his name in relief.

His truck slid to a stop outside the helicopter. He came flying out the door and ran to her side. "Tara Jean, are you hurt?"

She was so relieved, she couldn't speak at first. She swallowed hard and shook her head. "My seat belt is jammed. I can't get out."

He called back over his shoulder, "Get my knife out of the glove compartment!"

Opening the door, he stood beneath her. He was within reach. She didn't hesitate. She threw her arms around his neck, pulled him close and kissed him. He was surprised but not for long. He kissed her back. His lips were dry and warm, his arms even warmer as he wrapped them around her. She shivered in reflex and pulled him closer.

"I love you, Trace Leyton. I've loved you all my life," she murmured against his lips. She wanted to say more, but Trace kissed her again, stopping whatever else she'd meant to say.

Belter came up behind him. "I've got the knife."

Trace glanced back. "She's stuck. I'm going to catch her. You cut her loose from the top."

TJ suppressed her dread of more pain and gritted her teeth in preparation. Belter stepped up on the helo's skid and braced his foot. Leaning in, he sawed on the strap.

At long last, TJ broke free and fell into Trace's waiting arms.

Trace carried Tara Jean to his truck and nudged his chin at Belter, directing him toward the driver's seat. For someone who was so fiercely independent and brave, Tara Jean's slender frame felt fragile in his arms. She must be deeply frightened—or hurt—to let the words she'd just said slip out. That thought jolted him. He set her gently on the seat.

"Where are you hurt?"

"Just my ribs. I think they're bruised but not broken. I just couldn't breathe, tilted like I was. I couldn't move. When the gang came over the hill…" She gasped. "My gun." She turned to Belter, who was the closest to the damaged helicopter. "Grab my .22 from beneath the seat. We can't leave it there, and we have to go after

Denby's men. We have to find out where they are going."

Belter nodded and ran back through the pouring rain to fetch her gun. Trace was standing outside the door, too.

"We're not going after those men. We're getting you to a hospital."

"Honestly, Trace, I'm all right. The gang was just over that hill. I think they're gone now. I heard their motorcycles revving up. But they have all heavy weapons, including another AMR gun. That's what brought my helicopter down. We have to get up there and see where they've gone."

Trace stood outside the truck, rain sliding down his face.

Belter slid into the driver's seat and shook his head. "Seriously, if you're intent on standing in the rain, at least close the door so Tara Jean can warm up."

She turned to the agent. "Oh, not you, too. Seriously, what's wrong with calling me TJ?"

Belter shrugged. "Your name is too…"

"…pretty not to use it," she said, finishing with a shake of her head. "Seems I've heard that before."

Still, Trace stood outside the door.

"Trace, they might have Chad with them. They shot at me before I got a good look inside the barn. They could have been holding him there the whole time."

She was right. He hated to admit it, but he needed to see the direction they'd taken. It could be his last chance to save his brother. He motioned to TJ to move over and slid in. Then he slammed the door. "We're going to check out the hay barn, but as soon as we do, we're going back to the ranch."

"We can't risk losing them. As soon as we give Gomez their direction, I'll go to the hospital and let them give me a thorough examination, I promise."

But Trace knew Gomez was mopping up the Martinez operation and wouldn't be able to get here soon. By the time the agent arrived, Denby—and Chad— might be long gone.

Trace would not share that bit of info with Tara Jean. She'd never consent to go to the ranch if he did. But he and Belter could follow the gang—and they would.

He gave the agent a look over Tara Jean's head. "Follow their trail to the highway. We'll be able to see which direction they took from there. Following that route instead of the muddy roads will be our quickest route to the house anyway."

Belter spun the truck around, sending mud flying behind them again as the vehicle plowed up the hill. From the top, they could see the empty barn and the deep furrows the heavily loaded vehicle had made in the soggy ground—as well as the single tracks of multiple motorcycles.

The sight of the motorcycle tracks gave Trace a moment of hesitation. "How many motorcycles and men were there?"

Tara Jean was silent for a moment before she shook her head. "I don't know. It all happened so fast. Maybe ten or fifteen."

Trace processed this information. Ten or fifteen against the three of them—numbers they could not possibly handle. He and Belter alone couldn't take on this group. They would have to wait at the ranch for Gomez and his men.

Not even pausing, Belter drove the truck down the hill, carefully avoiding the furrows now filled with water. He sped into the curve as he turned down the rain-soaked dirt road headed south. Thankfully, beyond the hay barn, the road was a straight shot without hills and dips. Still, he hit a few bumps. Trace heard Tara Jean catch her breath as they jounced up and down. But she held back and never said a word as Belter rocked and slid at top speed down the muddy road.

At last, they came to the asphalt highway where the dirt road ended in a T. The rain had done a good job of clearing most of the tracks away, but there was enough mud left to see the truck and motorcycles headed west.

Belter turned onto it without pause. "Is this the way to the main highway?"

Trace nodded. "The intel about the Martinez shipment of drugs was a setup, a decoy, so Denby could get his weapons delivered. That truck is going to meet up with the rest of the gang, and I think I know where."

Belter nodded but didn't slow down. He sped down the highway at a pace too dangerous for the slick roads. But no one in the truck said a word.

Trace tried his cell phone, but the storm had temporarily knocked out all reception. Hopefully, when they reached the ranch, they'd be able to contact Gomez.

They soon reached the main highway. The muddy tracks disappeared beneath a multitude of other tracks.

Belter slapped the wheel. "Don't folks know there's a tornado watch? They're supposed to shelter in place."

Trace understood the agent's frustration but couldn't suppress his ironic tone. "Like we are?"

Belter smiled. Tara Jean's nod of agreement ended with a shiver. Trace could feel her beginning to shake beneath the blanket he'd pulled from behind the seat. With a rueful gesture, Trace pointed down the ranch's road. "Come on. Let's get Tara Jean back and into some dry clothes."

This time she didn't argue, and Trace was glad because he had another reason for getting back to the ranch. He was certain he knew where the gang might be headed, and time was of the essence.

It was a silent drive as they headed home. Trace tried to suppress his impatience. As soon as they pulled beneath the portico, Eva rushed out, followed by his mother.

"Oh, thank the Lord! I've been half out of my mind with worry."

Tara Jean climbed out of the truck and was immediately embraced by her mother. The hug resulted in Tara Jean groaning with pain.

"Sorry, Mom. My ribs are a little sore." Apparently, she was feeling the results of her crash. She sagged into her mother's embrace and stayed there.

"She needs some dry clothes and a trip to the hospital to get checked out," Trace told Eva.

Eva bundled her strangely compliant daughter toward the house. "I'll see to it."

As she turned away, Eva mouthed the words *thank you* over her shoulder. Trace nodded.

His mother touched his arm. "What about you? You're soaked to the skin."

"I'll get us some dry clothes. Tell Dad to meet me in his office in ten minutes."

Without another word, he hurried into his room to change clothes and to find a dry shirt for Belter. The agent entered the office at the same time as Trace returned. He tossed him the shirt.

Trace looked at his dad. "I don't know why I didn't think of it before, but when I saw those tracks leading south, I knew I was right. Denby's been holing up at the Baskinses' airfield."

His father nodded. "Of course. You checked it out and moved the women. The airfield is empty—it's the perfect location to hide the weapons."

"I left Agent Gomez and his men mopping up the raid. They can't get here fast enough, and with the storm, they'll be more delayed. I tried to get through to them, but I couldn't. If we're going to stop the gang, we have to be the ones to do it."

Belter nodded. "We'll do our best. There's five of us plus you. We'll manage."

His dad pulled a map from a side cabinet, spread it out on the desk and pointed to a road. "My guess is they took this. It cuts across the old Hastings property."

Trace shook his head. "It's a dirt road. I doubt they'd take the chance of getting stuck with their heavy load."

His dad straightened. "They paved it over last year.

The road cuts off fifteen minutes to the highway. They're probably already at the Baskinses' airstrip."

Trace exhaled. "You're right."

Dad nodded. "They'll use one of Tara Jean's planes and take off for Mexico as soon as it's clear."

Trace stared at his father over the desk. "We have to act quickly, Dad. See if you can get through to Gomez on the house's landline."

He nodded. Trace turned to Belter. "We'll use the ranch Jeep and cut across the pastures. It'll save us time."

His father grabbed the phone off his desk and began dialing. Trace opened the drawer where the keys to the gun locker were stored. He pulled out the rifles and handed all the ammo he could carry to Belter.

His father couldn't connect to anyone in Leytonville, so he tried the BPS headquarters in Del Rio. Someone came on the line, and his father updated him with the situation.

His father listened for a long while before saying, "Right. You want them to find out the gang's location but not take any chances until reinforcements arrive."

He looked at Trace's set features before turning back to the phone.

"We understand your directions, Commander, but I'm quite certain my son will do whatever it takes to save his brother."

The man said something, and his dad responded, "Roger that."

He hung up.

"What did he say?"

"He told you to use your discretion, and I agree. Do what you can, Trace, but capturing Denby is not worth another life. I don't want to lose two sons tonight."

In addition to his service revolver, Trace strapped on a shoulder holster. "Understood."

At that moment, the office door slammed open. Missy rushed into the room. Her wrists were bleeding, her hair was mussed and she had a white bandanna around her neck.

She ran straight to Trace and frantically grasped his shirt. "He took my baby, Trace. He has Bobby."

"Missy, what…"

Eva followed close behind. She was almost as frantic. "I was just chattering away to Tara Jean, working off my worry, I guess. I mentioned how happy Squirt will be to see her and how he and Bobby went to check on the horses after the storm. All of a sudden, she said the wrangler's name and ran out the door."

Tara Jean's mother wrung her hands. "I thought she was going to tell Squirt she was safe. I didn't know something was wrong. I just stood there, watching the bathtub fill. Tara Jean was so cold. All I wanted was to get her into it and warmed up. When she didn't come back, I went to the barn and found Missy tied up to a post. Handy took them all, Trace. Missy says he was gloating about how Denby's men couldn't get through, but he could drive right off the property and no one would stop him."

Trace squeezed his eyes shut. "It was Handy feeding Denby info all along."

Eva nodded. "He took Chad, too. He told Missy he

followed Chad from the barn the night of the attack. He hit him from behind and shoved him in his car. One of those men just drove it away with Chad unconscious in the back seat."

Missy burst into tears and clung to Trace. "My brother was after Bobby all along. He wanted to hurt me in the worst possible way, and now he has my baby. You know how he'll treat him, Trace. Help him. Please help him."

NINE

TJ sat in the passenger seat of Handy's small, dilapidated Toyota truck. Bobby sat on her lap, his face buried in her neck. His hot tears flowed down into her shirt unchecked. Squirt sat next to her, scrunched up as close to her as possible.

"He hurt my mommy," Bobby whimpered, his tearful words barely audible.

"It's all right," Squirt whispered to him. "TJ will take care of us."

The boys' murmured words made Handy laugh. "Yeah, sure she will. Just like she has so far."

TJ gritted her teeth, not daring to respond. Instead, she stroked Bobby's head and pressed it closer to her. "Your mama will be all right. I promise."

Missy was safe. They were the ones in danger. The minute Handy hit the main road and headed south, TJ realized where they were headed and why he'd brought her along. Denby and his gang might be able to use her pilot skills.

She tried to slow her breathing while her mind

raced. If she flew over the border with his cache of weapons, she and the boys would never return. They'd disappear and probably end up in Los Desaparecidos' killing field.

She closed her eyes. That would suit Denby's plan. It was the perfect way to hurt Missy and Trace…and maybe even Chad, if he was still alive.

Take the boys and everyone would suffer—and maybe never heal.

Her mother's words echoed in her head. Even true healing couldn't bring someone back from such a devastating blow. The loss of an innocent child. She would never recover from endangering Squirt's life. And Trace…losing his brother and a nephew he barely knew. Trace, Missy, her mother—all would pay for TJ's mistake.

And this was her fault. They were here because of her. She'd been so certain Chad was guilty, so focused on uncovering his lies, she'd ignored the signs around her. Squirt's dislike of the wrangler. Handy's aggressive tone toward Chad that night in the barn. His smirking smiles and underhanded comments not only made him unlikable but signaled his feelings of superiority…like he knew something they didn't know. But she had ignored the signals because she was so focused on Chad. Now they were caught. Trapped like animals in a cage.

Still, she wouldn't go down without a fight. She had to try to stop this. She looked at her captor. "How long have you hated the Leytons?"

He glanced her way and snorted. "As long as they've

lorded it over me…which is pretty much since we were kids. Don't tell me you didn't feel it, too. Trace treated you like trash when school started. I know. I watched it all."

"You watched Trace and I?"

"Come on. The whole school knew about you two. He made you a laughingstock."

TJ swallowed. "Maybe, but that was my business. What did they do to you? You've worked for them most of your adult life."

"Yeah, I have. And all that time, they treated me like I was just another hand. I worked my fingers to the bone for them and once in a while, if I was good, they'd toss me a bone like a dog."

His jaw tightened. "When I turn you three over, Denby's gonna pay me enough to buy my own horse ranch, far from here and the Leytons. All Bill wanted was his nephew. Now that I got him a bona fide pilot, I'm gonna ask for a bigger cut. You're a bonus he won't be expecting, and I'll make sure he pays for it."

So TJ had been right about Denby's motive. He wanted vengeance on everyone, including Chad. His target had always been Bobby. The youngster shivered in her arms, as if he understood the implications of his uncle's plans for him.

She'd been hoping she could convince Denby to leave the boys behind. With her as a hostage, he didn't need the youngsters. But it was useless. Denby wanted to hurt them. Any hope of making deals or promises would fail. Denby wanted to cause pain, and with all of them in his grasp, he could do the most damage.

She grasped Bobby tighter and put her arm around Squirt.

Please, Lord, forgive my stubborn willfulness. Show me Your Mercy. Help me get these little ones to safety... and if it pleases You, let me make things right with Trace.

Handy made the turn onto the dirt road leading to her house. He went so fast, the truck skidded across the wet pavement. The rain had stopped, but standing water and puddles were everywhere. The storm had passed, headed south—in the very direction Denby wanted to go.

Handy stopped at the top of the rise and looked down on her airstrip. Three black trucks and a semi surrounded her air tanker. TJ shook her head. The engine on that plane wouldn't run. They would have to delay their departure to load the cargo onto another plane. Maybe that would give Trace and Gomez time enough to get here...if Trace knew where Handy was taking them.

She remembered his words in the truck. He said he knew where Denby was. He must have figured it out when he saw the tracks on the highway. She hoped it was true. Their rescue depended on it.

"What are you smiling about?" Handy's rough voice grated across her nerves.

She didn't even realize she was smiling. "I'm just glad to see my planes are safe after the storm."

The man glanced her way once, then twice. TJ kept her gaze focused below and schooled her features into a blank expression.

Handy released the brake and drove down the hill, past the house, right onto the airstrip. Someone stepped away from the large plane and headed their way. Even with a full beard, TJ recognized Bill Denby's features twisted into a grimace-like smile. She would probably see his face in her nightmares for the rest of her life… or what little life might be left to her, anyway.

Handy pulled to a stop and motioned them out. TJ opened the truck door and hoisted poor Bobby onto the ground. He wouldn't even release her hand long enough for her to climb out. Squirt scooted out behind her and stepped in front of her. Blocking his hand from the view of the men behind him, he opened his palm— a silver horse bit with a leather strap rested there. He looked up at her meaningfully. TJ nodded and took his hand, firmly gripping the metal bit in hers.

"Have I ever told you, Squirt, you're the smartest boy I know?"

"Yes, ma'am," the youngster whispered, still gripping her hand as he spun around to face their captors.

"Boy, come here and greet your uncle." Bill Denby's gravelly voice made TJ shudder.

Bobby made a noise and scuttled closer to TJ.

"Boy! I said come here."

Bobby shook his head.

Afraid to ignite Denby's temper, TJ took a half step forward—only a half step because Bobby held her in such a tight grip she couldn't move. "Bobby," she said, lowering her voice, "do you know how brave you are?"

He shook his head, pressed against her waist.

"You and Squirt are the bravest boys I know. I

wouldn't want to be any place but right here with the two smartest and bravest boys in the world. Now let's go see that man."

Her words seem to give the little guy courage because he loosened his grip enough for TJ to take a full step. Gripping the hands of the boys, she walked closer to her lifelong enemy.

Bill Denby had aged. Hard living had left its marks on him. His skin was rough, wrinkled and pitted. His eyes were dark, and he had a scar that ran from the right side of his mouth to his ear, making a hairless track straight through his beard. His gaze focused on his nephew.

At last, he shook his head. "You look like your mama when she was your age." For just a moment, TJ thought Denby's tone softened.

Then he looked at TJ. "Well, TJ, you grew up." For the first time in memory, she didn't like the sound of someone using her nickname.

"You look a lot better than the scrawny kid I remember."

The tone of his voice, the sly, lascivious note, was designed to frighten her. It worked.

But she refused to show it. "I can't say the same for you. Looks like the friends you picked didn't care for your face."

His hand shot to the scar on his cheek, and his smile faded. "That smart mouth of yours hasn't changed a bit though. I'd still like to smash my fist into it."

He'd tried that when they were kids and failed. She

wanted to remind him of that fact, but she didn't dare push him. She had to consider the boys' safety.

Denby turned to Handy. "You did good bringing her. Head out with the boys, and when I have the money, I'll send for you all."

Handy shook his head and smiled with crooked teeth. "I don't think so, Bill. I'm coming with you on the plane."

"That's not the plan. Only Aldan is flying with me."

"The plans have changed."

Denby stiffened to his full height, and one fist curled.

Handy held up a hand. "Now Bill, don't lose that famous temper on me. I'm a quick thinker and fast on my feet. I've already proven my worth. You know I might be useful down in Mexico."

Denby hesitated. "Yeah, you might be. But don't make me regret changing my mind. Get those three loaded on the plane."

Handy walked to them and shoved Bobby away from TJ. "Let's go, crybaby. You're first."

TJ clenched the bit in her fist. If she got the chance, Handy would be the first to feel the metal resting in her palm.

She gripped Bobby and pulled him back into her embrace, then turned to Denby. "Bill, you can't seriously mean to fly into that storm." She gestured to the black clouds. "That's moving south. You can't fly into that. You'll crash."

"I'm sure you'd rather I stay here and wait for Agent Gomez's team, wouldn't you?"

Surprise swept over TJ, and she almost took a step backward.

"Yeah, I know all about Special Agent Gomez and his team. I will not sit here and wait to be shot. I'll take my chances with the storm. Get on the plane."

He turned and started to walk away. But she stopped him again, braving his short temper. She had to try. "At least leave the boys here. I'll fly you wherever you want to go, and I'll do a better job than any other pilot. I know this area better than most, and you'll have me as a hostage. You won't need them."

Denby turned slowly, and the look on his face was as vicious as she'd ever seen. "You don't get it, do you? I didn't come here just to get across the border. I could have made arrangements with other gangs anywhere along the border. I came here, to my hometown, to pay you all back."

It was just as TJ suspected, but she was stalling for time, so she acted surprised. "To get back at us? For what? We were your victims, not the other way around."

Denby spun and strode toward her. TJ took several steps back, dragging the boys with her. Denby only stopped when he was towering over her.

"There were only two people in this world I cared about, and those two betrayed me. Chad was my best friend until his kid brother got soft on you. Our first fight happened when Chad told me to lay off you 'cause Trace asked him to. We never fought, not once, until you came along. Then my best friend started seeing my sister behind my back. Imagine my surprise when he showed up."

He gestured to Bobby. TJ pressed one side of his head against her waist and covered his open ear, but she couldn't cover Squirt's ears. He turned shocked features on TJ. Desperate to stop Denby's cruel tirade, she blurted out, "It's not their fault! Don't make them pay for grown-up mistakes."

Denby shook his head and glared at her. "You're all going to pay. I'm making sure no one ever crosses me again. No one!"

Terrified, TJ clutched the boys and cringed. She'd never been face-to-face with such hatred and pain. She wished she could find a hole and crawl into it. She was certain Denby was going to strike her. Instead, he jerked his arm toward Handy.

"Get them out of my sight!"

He spun and strode away. Handy hurried toward them, chuckling as he went. "If I was you, I'd keep that pretty little mouth closed and not rile him anymore."

TJ exhaled in relief as he pushed them toward the back of the plane where men had just finished loading the last crate of weapons.

If Denby got that mad when confronted with the truth, what would he do when the engine of this plane wouldn't turn over?

TJ considered warning Handy and letting him break the truth to Denby when a man came running toward them from the house. Wait... From the house? Denby and his men were living inside her home, touching her things? She hadn't really considered that.

A wave of nausea swept over her, but it lasted only long enough for the man's shouted words to register.

"The police scanner is lit up! FBI agents and every cop within a fifty-mile radius is headed this way!"

Trace huddled behind the top of the hill with the five FBI agents. From what they could tell, there were about fifteen members of the gang against the five of them. Not great odds. But they needed to act. Denby and his men had almost completed loading all the crates of weapons onto a plane. Trace wasn't sure, but if he remembered correctly, the engine on that plane was nonfunctioning. If he was right, then the men would have to unload and move their cargo to another plane. That would give them more opportunities to find Chad and get to the others.

Tara Jean and the children stood in front of the cargo plane. The kids clung to her slender frame. Poor little Bobby wouldn't even look at Denby as he shouted at them. Suddenly, Denby marched toward them, yelling all the way. Trace gripped his pistol, but Belter put a restraining hand on his arm.

He knew he couldn't shoot, but he physically reacted to the threat to Tara Jean from that madman. He wanted nothing more than to run down the hill to protect her. But Tara Jean didn't back down. In fact, her spine straightened, and she faced Denby with her chin up. Desperate to move, he scooted back down off the rise and the men followed, except for one who stayed on guard at the top.

"As far as I can tell, there are two men in the house."

Belter nodded. "Roger that. The rest of the gang seems to be working on loading the weapons."

"I don't see Red Beard. That bothers me. I know he has to be here."

"Do you think they have Chad on the plane?"

Trace shook his head. "I don't know. My guess is Chad's with Red Beard, wherever that is."

If he's still alive.

Trace suppressed the thought. He couldn't think about that. For now, he had to believe Chad was alive. He had to or he wouldn't be able to put one foot in front of the other.

Belter spoke to his men. "I think our best option is to fan out. Pick a location. When we're all in place, we can begin working our way through the group to find the hostages. My hope is we can find them before the shooting starts."

Trace agreed. "I'll take the house, then move to the Quonset hut. Those are the most likely places they'd keep Chad."

Belter pointed to the closest agent. "You take the west side. I'll go east. We need to surround the airfield as much as possible."

Suddenly, the agent on guard spoke in low tones. "Get up here. Something is happening."

They scrambled on their bellies to the top, just in time to see a gang member running from the house down to the field. The last of his words drifted over the air.

Then Denby turned and bellowed across the field,

"Fire up and get out of here! We'll meet in Mexico in two weeks' time!"

Trace and Belter exchanged looks. Trace gave a shake of his head. "We can't stop them. The hostages have to be our priority."

Belter agreed. "Change of plans. I'll take the house. You get to the hut." He looked at the men. "Give us time to find the hostages. If some men leave, we have to let them go."

They all dipped their heads in agreement. Trace backed down the hill and ran around it. Thankfully, it was growing late. The storm's cloud cover made it gloomy, and the late afternoon hour created long shadows. He prayed it would shield him enough to get to the hut.

The gang was preparing to leave. He heard motorcycles revving and knew Belter's men would be itching to stop the gang members from escaping. That lent speed to his feet.

No time to wait.

He darted across the open road in full view of anyone on the field and dove into a gathering of mesquite bushes. The sharp needles of the bush scratched his skin and dug into him, but no shots were fired. He'd made it across. Most of the men must have been busy preparing to leave.

Now to get to the hut. Gathering his feet beneath him, he stayed low. Then he ran, arms and legs pumping, to the back side of the hut. He leaned against the metal wall, heart pounding and ears tuned to the shouting men and motorcycles. He couldn't see inside the hut, but if he didn't move, he would be in full view of the departing riders.

Taking two deep breaths, he lunged around the corner and ducked inside.

Chad sat in the middle of the hut, hands and feet bound to a metal chair with zip ties. His eye was swollen shut. His nose was bleeding, and his bottom lip was split open. His head was drooping. He'd been beaten, but Trace couldn't see any major wounds. A quick glance around the hut told Trace it was empty except for his brother. Shoving his gun into its holster, he ran across the room.

"Chad!" He knelt beside his brother. "Wake up! It's me."

"Trace?"

Chad was groggy but tried to focus on him. "Trace... Bobby. Bill's after Bobby. You have to stop him."

Relief swept through Trace. His brother was semi-coherent. "He's here, Chad."

Lunging to his feet, he looked around for something to cut the zip ties. "Bobby's here. Denby has him. We've got to get you loose so you can help me save him."

He found a razor blade holder on Tara Jean's workbench and snapped the zip ties apart. Chad leaned into him, too weak to hold himself up.

"Come on, Chad. You gotta move. We gotta get to them."

His brother stood on shaky legs. He wobbled and fell into Trace, who stumbled back, trying to balance them both.

At that moment, Red Beard walked into the hut. Bellowing his rage, he charged.

Trace didn't have time to draw his gun. He shoved Chad in the clear, just as Red Beard hit him at a full run. They both went flying and hit the ground hard.

Red Beard was on top of Trace. The burly man's weight knocked the breath out of him. He was stunned and, for a moment, couldn't move.

When he looked up, Red Beard was on his knees above him. His massive fist was raised high above his head, about to come down on Trace.

Suddenly, a metal bar swung across Trace's view. It hit Red Beard on the side with such force, it sent the man rolling. He hit his head on the side of the work-bench and didn't get up.

Trace turned. Chad was leaning on a five-foot metal bar. "Give me his gun and let's go get Bobby."

TJ watched men scramble. Motorcycle engines revved all around them and sped down the airstrip headed to the hill.

Only a few were left when Denby turned and headed their way. Handy shoved TJ and the boys. The gang leader gestured to Handy. "Go on. Get them in there and start the engine."

TJ knew they couldn't get on that plane. She halted her footsteps, desperate to find a way to get the boys free when someone shouted over the roar of motor-cycles.

"Bill!"

Denby halted and turned. Chad stepped out from

behind the Piper next to the Quonset hut. He had a revolver in his hand, pointed straight at Denby.

"You!" Denby cursed and drew a gun from behind
his back.

Handy stopped his progress and turned to run down
the ramp. TJ gripped the leather straps of the bit so that
the metal rested outside her knuckles. As he passed,
she grabbed his arm. Surprised, he turned toward her.
She raised her arm back and punched him in the jaw.
His head popped back, and he dropped to the ground
like a bag of rocks. TJ grabbed the boys and ran up the
ramp for cover inside the plane.

More shots exploded, some close, some far away.
TJ didn't know how many people were out there. But
if Chad was here, she hoped Trace was too. She just
needed to get the boys to safety and wait for him to
find them.

She hurried the boys around the cases of weapons
and didn't look back. When they reached the front of
the plane, she glanced out the cockpit window and almost stumbled. Chad had been shot. He was lying on
the asphalt with blood pooling around him. Denby was
nowhere in sight. Catching her breath, she looked away
and encouraged the boys to hurry.

If she knew Denby, he was probably close behind
them.

All the planes on this side of the airstrip were lined
up along the side, noses pointing out, and latched se-
curely to the ground. Her grandfather had set them
up this way years ago for his museum tours. Visitors
would enter the back of one plane and exit the front

hatch to continue the tour to the next plane. The setup worked perfectly for TJ right now. If they could reach the front hatch, they could climb down and run to the next plane, using the wheels for cover.

She ran to the cargo hatch and hefted it open. Her injured ribs twinged as she pulled the heavy door up and lowered her head to look beneath. Denby was nowhere in sight.

She motioned to Squirt. "Come on. You first. Climb down. Then I'll lower Bobby down to you. Both of you head over to the next plane. I'll be right behind you. Understand?"

Squirt nodded. TJ gripped his hands and lowered him down to the ground. Her ribs screamed in protest, but she ignored them. She had to get the boys away.

Squirt's feet touched the ground. She lifted Bobby down into Squirt's arms. It was a good thing neither of the boys weighed much because TJ didn't know how many more times she could do this. There were at least three more planes between them and the hangar where TJ could lock the doors and hide until help arrived.

Holding her breath, she sat down and slid off the edge of the hatch just as bullets tore through the back end of the plane. TJ landed with a jarring sensation that shook her to the core. She stifled her cry, but she need not have bothered. No one could have heard her over the roar of rapid firing bullets from Denby's Uzi and his shouts of rage as he fired at the plane, shredding it.

Lunging to her feet, TJ ran to the next plane. Squirt had already led Bobby there. He'd climbed up the wheelbase and leaped across the space to grasp the handle of the hatch. It flew open and Squirt dropped down just as TJ arrived.

"Good job! I said you were the smartest boy I know."

She lifted him high enough to grasp the edges of the hatch, and he pulled himself inside. Then TJ lifted Bobby to him. He gripped his little friend's hands but couldn't pull Bobby in on his own. TJ had to lift him. Then both boys pulled on her and dragged her into the plane as her strength began to wane. Inside, she climbed to her feet. They ran to the front of the plane as bullets ripped through the back end again. Denby wasn't wasting time searching for them. He continued his rampage, marching his way down the field and firing, destroying her planes and everything inside them.

He was getting closer and closer. Thankfully, the next plane was lower to the ground. Squirt climbed in without her help. She needed all her strength to lift Bobby and then herself inside. She lay on the floor, breathing deeply as the boys ran to the front and lifted the hatch.

"Come on, TJ!"

She climbed to her feet. Only one more plane to go before they reached her Piper. A good thing. She wasn't sure she could do any more.

The boys hopped to the ground. TJ slid down behind them as they ran to the next aircraft. This was the last empty cargo plane. The next was her small Piper, too small to climb through. They'd use it for cover before they made a dash to the back of the Quonset hut.

TJ sighed with relief and climbed to her feet, trudging through the derelict, empty plane. Just then, an explosion rocked them so furiously, they all tumbled to the floor of the plane. They climbed to their feet, hurried to the cockpit window and stared out. Massive flames shot out from the top of the Quonset hut, and black smoke billowed high into the sky.

Trace surveyed the airfield. Sporadic gunfire sounded from different parts of the area. Belter and his men were still under fire someplace near the hill. But all the trucks and motorcycles were gone. Most of Denby's gang had abandoned him. He was the only one left, but Trace didn't know where he was.

Chad lay on the asphalt, but Trace couldn't reach him without going into the open and he couldn't risk it. He had to get to Tara Jean and the boys. He promised Chad he would get Bobby away.

Trace dodged behind the damaged Piper and looked around before he ran to the next plane. He was sure that was where Tara Jean and the boys were hiding. He ducked beneath the plane's belly and popped the hatch up. It was low enough to the ground that he could stick his head in.

The boys screamed in surprise and lunged into TJ's arms. She gasped and pulled them back into the shadows. When TJ realized it was him, she sobbed with relief and dropped to the floor of the plane. Trace holstered his service pistol before he pulled himself inside the plane and closed the hatch. He hurried to where they were huddled.

"Are you all right?"

Squirt, who didn't give hugs easily, threw himself

into Trace's arms. "I knew you were out there some-where."

Bobby clung to Tara Jean, who looked drawn, pale and exhausted.

"Is anybody hurt?" he repeated, his relief at finding them shifting to concern as Tara Jean didn't answer.

At last, she took a deep breath and seemed to re-cover. "We're just tired. Otherwise, we're fine. How did you find us?"

"It wasn't hard with Denby shooting planes all the way down the runway."

Tara Jean gave a frustrated shake of her head. "Why did he stop?"

"He figured out you were headed to the Quonset hut and took it out instead. He was shredding it with his Uzi and must have hit your welding tank. It went up like a rocket. Red Beard is unconscious in there." He gave a disgusted shake of his head. "I doubt he could have survived the blast. Denby took out his own man."

"Where is he now?"

"I don't know. Last I saw, he was flying through the air. He was closer to the hut than I was, and the explo-sion blew him away."

"Do you think he's hurt?"

Trace shook his head. "Not bad enough to stop him, if that's what you're hoping. He's out there somewhere, gathering his strength."

TJ pulled herself together and stood. "We have to get out of here while we can."

Trace shook his head. "The only way out of here now is to reach that truck by the house. We have to cross the open airstrip. We can't do that until I find Denby."

He walked to the closest window and peeked out.

Tara Jean came to stand beside him. "Chad's still out there on the ground."

"I know. I can't reach him."

"Is he…"

"I don't know." Trace stopped her before she could say the words. He couldn't stand the fact that his brother was lying out there on the asphalt and he couldn't help him. But Chad made him promise to get his son safely out of Denby's hands. And Trace intended to keep that promise.

"The Piper is right beside us, Trace. Let's get the boys over there and I'll fly us out of here."

"We can't. The explosion from the hut sent a piece of metal flying through the front windshield and the control panel. I don't know what kind of damage it did, and we'd be too exposed trying to pull the shrapnel out."

He gave his brother's inert body one more glance before looking toward the house where Eva's truck sat. "Does your mom still keep her keys in the visor?"

Tara Jean nodded.

He scanned the scene outside the window one more time. "All right. This is what we're going to do. Get the boys. Go around the back side of the hut. The smoke and flames should hide you from view. Make your way up the hill. Cross the road there. It's the shortest route to the house. Go straight to the truck and get out of here. I'm going to distract Denby. I'll move out onto the airstrip and keep him looking my way."

"You'll be a sitting duck."

"It's our only chance."

She shook her head. "And if Denby shoots you, then who'll stand between him and the boys?" She shook her head again. "No, I'm the one who has to distract him while you get the boys away."

"You're injured. You could barely muster the strength to walk over here. I have a better chance of surviving than you do."

She was silent for a moment longer before she grabbed his arm. "The gyrocopter, Trace. Was it damaged?"

Hope flared to life, and he racked his brain, trying to remember. It was tied to the same concrete ring as the Piper. He'd been so disheartened to see Chad lying on the tarmac, he had paid little attention to the small gyro.

"I… Yes. It looked undamaged. The Piper protected it, I think."

"I'll get in it and head down the runway in the opposite direction. He'll never see or hear you making your way to the truck."

He hesitated, but she squeezed his arm. "You know I'm right. You are the boys' only chance. You have to let me do this."

Trace stared at her. She was right. He knew it and he hated it. His gaze was drawn to the boys, standing in the shadows. Squirt's arm was around Bobby's shoulders, and Bobby's arm was around Squirt's waist. They clung together, their hair plastered to their foreheads with sweat, their cheeks bright red from the run through the planes, and both their gazes were wide-eyed. They'd been so brave and tried so hard, those two. Everything had happened so fast. He didn't have time to think, but his brother was down, shot, and he'd promised to protect his son. Still, if Tara Jean went out there, they might not have another chance.

He didn't want to leave her without telling her exactly how he felt.

Wrapping his hand around the back of her neck, he pulled her toward him and kissed her, hard and with enough tenderness to last a lifetime they might not have.

"I love you, Tara Jean Baskins. I've loved you since we were kids working on these planes together. I don't know what the future holds for us or where we'll go from here. I only know you need to come back to me. You have to come back to me. I'm only half alive without you."

He kissed her again with all his pent-up fear and love.

She gripped the hand holding her neck and squeezed. "I'll come back. We have too much to settle between us. You know I won't let that happen."

He gave her a brief smile. "Yes, I do know that about you."

He gave her another kiss, then turned to the youngsters. "Let's go, boys. We've got one more run ahead of us."

He opened the hatch and slipped down. A quick glance around the area told him Denby was nowhere in sight. He waited a moment longer, just to make sure the madman wasn't waiting for them to step out of the plane. At last, he motioned for Bobby to step forward. He lifted him down and tucked him behind the white wheelbase.

"Stay there and don't move."

Bobby's head bobbed vigorously. Trace reached up for Squirt, who had already seated himself on the edge of the hatch. He slid down into Trace's arms, followed by Tara Jean. Once the boys were sheltered behind the massive wheel of the plane, he drew his pistol, gripped it and slipped the safety off.

He gave the whole airstrip one last glance before nodding to Tara Jean.

TJ crouched low. When Trace gave her the signal, she dashed across the open space to the tethered gyrocopter. All the way across, her back itched as if she expected a bullet to hit her at any moment. But she made it to the tethered gyrocopter without incident. The heat from the flaming hut was almost unbearable and her hands slipped off the metal ratchet of the tether. She could barely grip it. She bent to reach out and a shot zinged past her. She glanced up to see Denby standing beside the hut.

"Duck!" Trace shouted behind her. She dropped to the ground as he fired multiple shots that drove Denby back behind the flaming building. On the ground, she gripped the tether, braced her feet against the cement block and pulled the tether loose. Lunging to her feet, she pushed the gyro clear of the Piper. All the time, her back burned, expecting a bullet to hit her at any moment. As soon as the gyro was free, she and climbed inside. The plexiglass-enclosed cockpit was so hot, it took her breath away. But she didn't hesitate. She flipped the engine switch. It turned over as smooth as glass and TJ sighed with relief. But the gyro needed plenty of runway to gain altitude. She might not get that time with Denby so close.

She had an idea. Heat had buckled the back door of the hut, and black smoke billowed out. She turned the controller of the gyro so that the small rotor on the tail end sent the smoke billowing where she had just seen Denby. That might keep him busy long enough for her to get far out of his range.

It worked. Acrid smoke blew toward the back of the hut. In a few short moments, Denby ran from behind the curtain of black smoke. She couldn't hear over the gyro engine, but by his physical gestures, she could tell he was coughing. He wiped at his eyes—for one long moment, he was out in the open, providing a perfect shot for Trace. She turned to look for him. Trace and the boys had already run to the front of the hut and were making their way up the hill to safety. She breathed another sigh of relief.

The black cloud blew across the runway and obscured her view of Denby. She lost him and didn't know where he was or what he was doing. She feared he might be headed back to where Trace and the boys were. But suddenly, he dashed out of the acrid cloud and cut across the open area toward the asphalt of the airstrip. He was moving sideways to get ahead of TJ. If he ran fast enough, he would be in the middle of the runway, right in front of her. She pumped the controls. The little gyro jumped, but it was hard going in the muddy dirt, and she had a long way to go before she reached the pavement.

Denby was going to get ahead. And he would have a clear shot at her. If she turned to go in the opposite direction, he would be facing Trace and the boys. She dared not point his gaze in that direction. She couldn't risk him turning his wrath on them. All she could do was keep going and pray he would miss her.

She kept her foot pressed to the pedal. The little copter was going as fast as the engine would go. She felt a little lift, but not enough to get her above Denby. He turned twenty feet ahead and faced her straight on. He lifted the Uzi and an ugly smile split his features. Tears streamed down his face from the smoke. Using an elbow, he wiped one side, then the other. All the while, he walked toward her with that evil grin taunting her. Then he took aim.

There was nothing TJ could do.

Suddenly he dropped the Uzi. Blood appeared on his white T-shirt beneath his black vest. It blossomed like a flower, spreading quickly. Shocked, he spun and tried to raise the Uzi again. Another shot hit him square in the chest and sent him flying backward. He fell flat on the ground with such force, the Uzi flew ten feet away.

TJ looked to the side. Chad stumbled toward the man who had been his best friend. Blood streamed down his arm from his shoulder, and he looked as if he could barely put one foot in front of the other. But he was alive...at least, for the time being. As TJ watched, his knees buckled, and he slumped to the ground again. She killed the gyro's engine and coasted to a stop.

Throwing open the cockpit door, she ran to where Denby's Uzi lay on the ground. She was afraid he might rise again so she picked the weapon up. Then she hurried over to the man who had destroyed her family home and almost killed her.

His eyes were wide open. Denby was dead.

She spun and ran to Chad. His shoulder was bleeding profusely. She fell to her knees beside him and cradled him in her arms.

"Bobby…is Bobby okay?"

TJ tugged his shirt loose, tore the buttons open and folded the bottom half over the bleeding spot on his shoulder. "Trace got them away. Chad…you saved my life."

He closed his eyes and murmured, "Good. Glad to do something right."

He slumped in TJ's arms just as a border-patrol helicopter flew over and FBI cars came down the hill, lights flashing and sirens blasting.

TEN

TJ sipped her coffee in the morning sun while standing outside her home on the patio. The scent of her mother's roses drifted up to her, sweet and soothing. The rose bed was one thing Denby's men had not destroyed. They had torn up the garden and wrecked the house, smashing furniture and dishes. They'd shot bullets into the walls and pretty much did damage everywhere possible. The only things they hadn't destroyed were her mother's roses and her radio and weather equipment, which they'd used to track the law-enforcement activities during their encampment.

Most of Denby's men had been captured or shot by Belter and his fellow agents. Pinned down as she was by Denby, she'd been unaware of the massive gun battle around her home. Now she was more than aware of how heated the battle had been. Many of Denby's men had been wounded, and Agent Belter had suffered a shot to the leg.

The incoming law-enforcement officers captured Denby's men who had attempted to escape in their vehicles and motorcycles. Surprisingly, many of them talked. The gang leader had recently hired them, and they owed him no loyalty. They laid out their activities of the last few days before the attack.

Denby had broken up the cases of arms and hidden them in different locations, then kept moving them as needed. Chad's vigilant searches had driven them from all their other hiding places. The airstrip was their last resort. Apparently, they'd arrived at the Baskinses' place just one day before the raid on Jose Martinez's shop. Denby had worked with Los Desaparecidos to throw off the law-enforcement agencies so he could get his weapons out of the States. Los Desaparecidos wanted to buy his weapons as badly as he wanted to sell them.

Their efforts had given border-patrol officers their first good link to the Mexican gang. They had found the van used in the attempt to kidnap Missy and Bobby inside a derelict semi at the back of the auto shop. Martinez and most of his employees had been arrested, giving the agency its first breakthrough with the gang.

Chad and the other injured men had been medevaced to local hospitals. Thankfully, Belter and Chad were doing well. Her mother told her that Missy spent most of her days at the hospital with him. She and Bobby had returned to their own home because it was closer to the hospital for their visits.

That had made TJ happy. It was the only bright spot in her days because the rest of her life was in shambles.

Even though Denby's men had been in her home

less than forty-eight hours, they'd done as much damage as possible, and the gun battle had finished their work. The house was unlivable. In fact, Eva and Squirt were still at the Leyton ranch. TJ had returned to begin the cleanup. She'd eked out a small living area for herself, but it would take months to make the house truly habitable again.

She surveyed her ruined airfield. It would take years to restore that…if it ever could be restored. Four of her grandfather's planes were destroyed beyond repair. Thankfully, her grandfather's favorite, his Kittyhawk, was on the other side of the field, away from Denby's rampage. But the four others, including her Piper, needed massive, expensive repairs. Her workshop was a smoking rubble, and her helicopter was still buried in mud on the Leyton ranch.

She had insurance, of course, but the damage was so great, she had little hope of bringing the airstrip back to its former operational level. All her dreams of creating a museum in her grandfather's name were gone. In fact, she wasn't sure how she was going to support herself or her mother and Squirt. If she didn't find a way, her mother's bid to become Squirt's foster parent might not go through.

TJ needed to do something. She *had* to find a way. But right now, she was too dispirited to think.

Trace had not returned since he flew away on the BPS helicopter with his brother. He hadn't called or contacted her in almost three weeks. She heard from her mother that he'd been given a commendation and sent on some trips to the state capital and then to the federal offices in Washington.

She was glad. He deserved that. But she would like to have known he hadn't forgotten her. She'd hoped the kiss and the last words he said to her on the plane were real. She hoped he really loved her. But as the days and weeks passed, she was beginning to believe they were words born of fear and trauma.

Her mother said forgiveness was a process. She knew that was true because she was having a hard time forgiving herself. She didn't feel she deserved it, and she blamed herself for the way things had ended. She was certain if she'd worked more closely with Chad, been more accepting, they might have gotten to Denby sooner, before Handy kidnapped her and the boys.

She couldn't go back and change that now, but she was trying to break down her walls, trying to trust a little more. It was a difficult process for her. She'd kept most people at arm's length for so long, she wasn't sure she knew how to do anything else. Relationships were a new and scary thing for her. Missy and Chad had both made room for her in their new life. She hoped Trace was working on doing that too. It was all she could hope for now. It was all she had left. She'd lost everything else.

Sighing, she poured the rest of her coffee in the roses, climbed inside her truck and drove it out to her Piper. Pulling heavy gloves off the seat, she climbed out and surveyed the damage. She pulled the metal out of the windshield and tossed it into the back of her truck. She swept the glass out of the cockpit and into bags, then moved to the next plane. The tail end was shredded, so she pulled away the useless parts and stacked ones that could be reused inside the aircraft. It was slow, hot work. Sweat pooled on her forehead and dripped down her back. She felt discouraged and wanted to quit, but she had no place else to go, nothing more to do, so she kept at it.

Close to noon, she heard a vehicle. Happy for the breather, she stopped. Raising a gloved hand to shield her eyes from the sun, she recognized Trace's truck coming down the hill. Her heart leaped with hope but immediately sank again.

Of course, he would stop by now when she was hot, sweaty and dirty. Couldn't even one thing go her way?

Sighing, she picked up another piece of scrap metal and tossed it into the back of her truck. Trace pulled up and climbed out of his vehicle. He looked clean and cool, and oh so handsome in jeans and a T-shirt. It only made her feel grimier.

She picked up another scrap piece and tossed it with a little more frustration.

He gestured to the damaged plane. "How goes the battle?"

She shook her head. "It's a battle all right. It'll take an army to get this place back in shape."

Trace nodded. "I'm sorry I haven't contacted you. I've been pretty occupied."

She picked up more debris. "My mom told me. She said the BPS flew you to Washington."

"Yeah, and while I was there, I met with a few of our representatives."

She paused. "You plan on taking Chad's place in politics?"

He chuckled. "Hardly. I have other ideas. I was just taking advantage of my father's connections."

"I see." She went back to collecting debris.

"I hope you know I meant what I said on the plane—"

"Don't, Trace. You don't have to explain. I know it was just emotion talking. Just a spur of—"

"Tara Jean, for once, will you stop trying to take charge? Stop talking and let *me* tell *you* how *I* feel?"

Her breath caught. He was right. After three weeks of apologizing to the Lord and promising to do better, she'd slipped right back into her old habit of controlling everything…especially things that might hurt. And Trace was definitely someone who could hurt her.

Trace shook his head, jerked a folded paper out of his jeans pocket and handed it to her. "Here."

Pulling off her gloves, she tucked them under her arm and unfolded the paper. It was a check made out to her, and it was a substantial amount. "What's this?"

"The reward for helping to capture Denby and his gang."

"Wow… I didn't expect this. It's a lot of money." She shook her head. "Still…it won't make much of an impact on rebuilding my airstrip."

"No, it won't rebuild your place. But it'll help buy a new helicopter, and you're going to need it to fly back and forth from our home on Lake Amistad."

"Our home—" TJ was so shocked she let the check flutter from her fingers.

Trace lunged forward and snatched it out of the air. "At last, you're silent." He grinned. "Yes, our home. It'll just be my trailer for now. But we're going to build a large facility, big enough for a youth center, right here next to your grandpa's house. I got support from two Texas representatives, and the governor's office is completely behind us. They say a youth center is exactly what this part of Texas needs. Your mom and mine are going to manage the facility. Mom wants to spend more time at home with her newfound grandson, and this was the perfect solution."

TJ couldn't keep up. Her mind was whirling, leaving her speechless—maybe for the first time in her life.

"I have our first resident in mind. He pulled a knife on me at the Martinez shop. But he's just a kid, a runaway who was scared senseless. I've been talking to his lawyer, asking him to put in an appeal to go easy on him."

He shrugged. "I don't know if it'll work, but he's just the kind of kid you could reach—a total misfit."

Still, TJ couldn't speak.

"So, what do you think? Will an army of troubled teenagers working and learning a craft be enough to rebuild your airstrip?"

She nodded, her head bobbing back and forth.

"Great. To move forward, all I need is the camp leader to agree to marry me and the deal will be sealed."

Before he even finished speaking, TJ leaped forward. Trace caught her in the air, and she wrapped her legs around him.

"Yes! Yes! A million times, yes!"

Trace smiled. "I knew you couldn't keep quiet much longer."

"Kiss me and I promise to stay very quiet."

He lowered his head and did just that.

* * * * *

Dear Reader,

I seem to have a surprising pulse on current news. Two years ago, *Killer Harvest*, my story about a virus decimating the world's crops, came out the month our country went into lockdown. My next book, *Vanished in the Mountains*, was about missing Native American women. It came out one month before the government launched an investigation into that exact situation. Two years ago, I picked a little Texas border area for a story about the theft of heavy arms. Who knew little Del Rio, Texas, would soon play such a large part in our news? As I tell you about these interesting connections, I hope you are smiling as much as I am!

I am part of a retirement community and am fortunate to know many people of fascinating backgrounds. Two of my friends are Vietnam war pilots who went on to fly planes and helicopters in civilian life. One was a commercial airline pilot. The other flew helicopters in air rescue operations, including the Mount St. Helens eruption. I've spent many afternoons enjoying their friendship and listening to their amazing stories. I owe them the inspiration for my story.

If you are interested in hearing more about my travels and adventures, be sure to sign up for my newsletter at www.subscribepage.com/c7i1q9.

Blessings!
Tanya Stowe

COMING NEXT MONTH FROM
Love Inspired Suspense

EXPLOSIVE REVENGE
Rocky Mountain K-9 Unit • by Maggie K. Black
After months of someone sabotaging their K-9 unit, Sargent Tyson Wilkes and K-9 Echo must scramble to uncover the culprit before their unit is disbanded. But when all signs point to a link with Detective Skylar Morgan's drug case, will working together be enough to stop the criminal...and keep them alive?

FORCED TO FLEE
by Terri Reed
Discovering a family secret instantly marks reserved banker Abby Frost as the target of a vicious cartel searching for her father. Tasked with keeping her safe, can US Marshal Jace Armstrong help Abby find the answers that she's looking for about her true identity before she falls into the crime ring's clutches?

SERIAL THREAT
Emergency Responders • by Valerie Hansen
A series of murders in her small Missouri town leads police officer Emily Zwalt straight to old friend and attorney, Noah Holden. With connections to all the victims, Noah's the main suspect. He'll have to enlist Emily's aid to unmask the real killer before they can strike again.

CHRISTMAS HOSTAGE
by Sharon Dunn
Taken hostage by bank robbers, security expert Laura Devin suspects one of the thieves is not who he appears to be. And when undercover FBI agent Hollis Pryce is forced to blow his cover to free Laura, he'll risk everything to assist her escape from the Montana mountains and the criminal mastermind hunting them.

TRACKED THROUGH THE MOUNTAINS
by Rhonda Starnes
When FBI profiler Sawyer Eldridge receives chilling threats from a serial killer who abducts his half-sister for revenge, he enlists bodyguard Bridget Vincent to track down the murderer. Except Bridget's also on the hit list and saving them both might not be possible...

ABDUCTION RESCUE
by Laurie Alice Eakes
Desperate to find his missing sister, Ethan McClure seeks out private investigator Melissa "Mel" Carter—only to be attacked right outside her agency's door. Though she's reluctant to help after her last case turned violent, Mel won't turn Ethan away. But can they avoid becoming pawns in the abductor's dangerous game?

SPECIAL EXCERPT FROM

LOVE INSPIRED SUSPENSE
INSPIRATIONAL ROMANCE

An FBI agent who is undercover as a bank robber
must risk his cover to keep a teller alive.

Read on for a sneak preview of
Christmas Hostage *by Sharon Dunn,*
available October 2022 from Love Inspired Suspense!

Even before the shouting and the woman's scream, Laura
Devin sensed that something was wrong in the lobby of
First Federal Bank. The bright morning conversation
between bank employees stopped abruptly, but it was
what she saw on her computer screen that told her they
were in the middle of a bank robbery. All the alarms and
cameras had been disabled, just like with the other small-
town banks that had been robbed in the last two years.

Her back was to the open door in the room next to the
lobby, where she was working at a computer. When she
whirled her chair around, she could only see the back of
one of the tellers. Then she saw a flash of movement on
the other side of the counter.

"This is a bank robbery! Do as I say, and no one will
die here today!"

Even if one of the tellers had time to push the silent
alarm, it had been disabled. The police would not show up.

Laura's gaze jolted to her purse across the room, where her phone was. The door was open. If she went for it, they might see her. Closing the door would alert the robbers to her presence that much faster. But she had no choice.

She sprinted across the carpet and grabbed her phone, pressing 911.

"Hey, there's somebody in that room! Get her!"

The operator came on the line. "What is your emergency?"

"Bank robbery—"

A hand went over her mouth. She dropped the phone before the thief could grab it from her. He must have seen that she was making a call, or at least heard the phone when it landed on the carpet. And yet, he didn't tell her to pick it up. Maybe it was still on and the operator could hear what was happening.

He whispered in her ear, the fabric of the ski mask he wore brushing over her cheek. "It's going to be okay. Just do what they say."

Don't miss
Christmas Hostage *by Sharon Dunn.*
*Available wherever Love Inspired Suspense books
and ebooks are sold.*

LoveInspired.com

LISEXP0822

IF YOU ENJOYED THIS BOOK, DON'T MISS NEW EXTENDED-LENGTH NOVELS FROM LOVE INSPIRED!

In addition to the Love Inspired books you know and love, we're excited to introduce even more uplifting stories in a longer format, with more inspiring fresh starts and page-turning thrills!

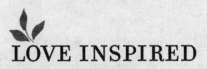

Stories to uplift and inspire.

Fall in love with Love Inspired—inspirational and uplifting stories of faith and hope. Find strength and comfort in the bonds of friendship and community. Revel in the warmth of possibility, and the promise of new beginnings.

LOOK FOR THESE LOVE INSPIRED TITLES ONLINE AND IN THE BOOK DEPARTMENT OF YOUR FAVORITE RETAILER!

LITRADE0622

LOVE INSPIRED

Stories to uplift and inspire

Fall in love with Love Inspired—
inspirational and uplifting stories of faith
and hope. Find strength and comfort in
the bonds of friendship and community.
Revel in the warmth of possibility and the
promise of new beginnings.

Sign up for the Love Inspired newsletter
at **LoveInspired.com** to be the first
to find out about upcoming titles,
special promotions and exclusive content.

CONNECT WITH US AT:

 Facebook.com/LoveInspiredBooks

Twitter.com/LoveInspiredBks